THE RAT CATCHER'S ORPHAN

VICTORIAN ROMANCE

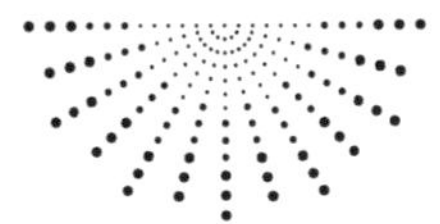

JESSICA WEIR

JOIN MY NEWSLETTER

WELCOME TO MY VICTORIAN WORLD

I am delighted that you are reading one of my Victorian Romances. It is a pleasure to share it with you. I hope you will enjoy reading them as much as I enjoyed writing them.

I would like to invite you to join my exclusive Newsletter. You will be the first to find out when my books are available. Join now, it is completely FREE and I will send you The Foundling's Despair FREE to read.

~

You can find all my books on Amazon, click the yellow follow button and Amazon will let you know when I have new releases and special offers.

Much love,

Jessica

CHAPTER ONE

"Sooner or later, I will have to speak to Mrs Coleman about this dreadful girl. Really, Rupert, this must be absolutely the last time we employ an orphan," Mildred Collins said in a whisper so loud that Jane knew she was meant to hear it.

"Did we ever employ an orphan before this one?" Rupert Collins asked, not even bothering with the pretence of a whisper.

Jane Ashford, the orphan in question and the maid in Rupert and Mildred Collins' home for almost a year, made a very good pretence of not hearing a word her employers said. Instead, she continued to build a fire in the grate of the drawing room. Her hands were shaking a little as she did her best to make a neat and symmetrical pyramid out of the coals.

To Jane, this seemed like a ridiculous, pointless waste of time. Why on earth would anybody need an unlit fire to look so perfect when, at any moment, they might strike a match and have the whole thing devoured by flames? It was just another quirk of the upper classes as far as she could see, and it strangely made her glad that she was not among their number.

Of course, being an impoverished orphan who had been edged out of the orphanage at just twelve years of age was not a particularly comfortable set of circumstances either. Jane had been picked by Mildred Collins. The woman's harsh glare had surveyed the short line of terrified girls, all of a similar age, in order to pick one whom she thought at least looked clean and decent.

Jane hadn't forgotten that day in the year and a half which followed, nor was she ever likely to forget it. She had felt like one apple in a box of apples at the market, with the prospective buyer studying her and all the rest at close quarters. At the time, she imagined being picked up out of the box and turned over and over in Mildred Collins' hands while the woman checked for blemishes. It had been a horrible experience, a dehumanising experience, and Jane had decided there and then that she would never like the woman. As the year had passed by and Jane had reached the great age of thirteen and a half, nothing had changed; she still did not like Mildred Collins, only now she had more and more reasons in her experience for that feeling.

"My dear Rupert, would you look at the dreadful state of those coals!" Mildred said in a high-pitched whine. "Really, it will be a mercy when the whole thing is set alight, won't it?"

"I never saw anything so shoddy, my dear, never." Rupert spoke in a somewhat deeper version of Mildred's whine.

Still, Jane knelt before the fireplace and continued to work. She felt humiliated, that dreadful sensation of being watched making her suddenly clumsy. Her hands were shaking with anger as she wondered if that awful couple had anything more in common between them than their cruelty.

"Girl, girl?" Mildred began in a determined tone.

"Rupert, what is her name again?" she said in that *out loud but under the breath* way, a style that was all her own.

"It is Jane, isn't it? Yes, it is Jane," Rupert added.

Jane bit down hard on her bottom lip. They both knew very well what her name was, but this was just one more tool in their upper-class box; it was designed to dehumanise her further still. What on earth did these dreadful people get out of such games? Slowly, Jane turned her head.

"Mrs Collins?" she said in a respectfully enquiring tone.

"No, no, do not look at me!" Mildred said, her eyes lighting up with glee. "There, now look what you have done!"

Jane turned back to look at the fireplace and saw that the tongs she was using had knocked the carefully placed coals all over the grate when she'd looked around at her mistress. It made her suddenly angry; it was all so unnecessary. Why couldn't they have just left her alone to get on with her work in peace? But no, they had to irritate her, anything to get their little bit of sport. Well, if that was where they found their joy, at least Jane could be glad that she was herself and not either one of them.

"I'm sorry, Mrs Collins," Jane said with practised deference as she began to rearrange the coals.

"At this rate, it will be dark before the fire is lit!" Mrs Collins said as if this was the greatest problem life had ever thrown at her; perhaps it was.

Jane could hear the enjoyment in the foul woman's voice, and it was all she could do to stoically re-stack the coals. This little piece of enjoyment was also contrived, so determined, and it made Jane angry. So angry that she closed her eyes and imagined striking Mrs Collins with the tongs.

She imagined Mrs Collins falling backwards in surprise, her peculiarly peach coloured hair, hair which must once have been a much more vibrant red, entirely disarranged as the mobcap she wore about the house when they didn't have visitors flew off. The image amused Jane a little and was just enough to break the anger. Jane needed this position and knew that her employers were capricious enough to dismiss her for the smallest of crimes. Losing her temper enough to even mildly complain about her treatment would certainly be enough to see her out on the streets. If only any other household in all of London had come to the orphanage that day looking to hire a maid. If only everything didn't feel so insecure, so uncertain.

Of course, Jane Ashford wouldn't be the only servant in London who felt as if her position was insecure, she knew that was the truth. However, nothing felt steady to Jane in that house as her employers see-sawed from cruelty to sense and then back again. But how would she escape them? If Jane were to leave and the Collins's didn't want her to go, Mrs Collins would simply not give her a reference. Jane knew that to have worked somewhere for more than a year and come out with no reference would make other households dubious of employing her. Oh, yes, Jane felt trapped all right.

Mr and Mrs Collins maintained their positions in the drawing room and watched Jane like hawks until the fire was finally set. Jane took a small cloth out of the pocket of her apron and wiped her hands clean before rising to her feet and getting ready to leave the room.

"Well, light it, girl," Rupert Collins said, shaking his head and tutting.

"Yes, sir." Jane reached for the box of matches on the mantle shelf. She struck one and lit the tag of paper she had left poking out between the coals. It was an easy lighting point. She gave it a moment or two before rising, seeing how well the fire took hold. She'd done a good job, whatever that miserable pair said.

"Will that be all?" Jane asked, her respectful tone so determined that it almost wasn't respectful at all. Still, she couldn't help but think that her privileged employers were too dull-witted to notice.

"Yes, that will be all," Mrs Collins said coolly.

Wasting no time, Jane hurriedly bobbed a small curtsy and headed for the door. As she reached it, she heard a clatter and a laugh and turned to see that Rupert Collins had used the poker in the fire to disarrange all the coals Jane had so painstakingly arranged. The laughter was Mildred's, clearly impressed by her husband's stupidity; what dreadful, privileged, pointless lives these people led.

"Would you just look at her, no better than she ought to be!" Mrs Coleman said with an angry click of her tongue.

Jane looked at her cautiously, then looked behind her. Mrs Coleman hardly ever spared her a word and certainly not in conversation. She gave her instructions, looked on disapprovingly, and that was that.

"Mrs Coleman?" Jane said in a quiet voice, certain that she must surely be mistaken; Mrs Coleman conversing with her? It was unheard of.

"Her, Miss Emma Talbot's maid! No better than she ought to be, I said!" She tipped her head in the direction of the window which looked out over the servants' yard beyond.

Jane followed her gaze to where a very fine-looking young woman was talking to Glyn Billington, the lad who delivered fruit and vegetables for the greengrocer.

Did Mrs Coleman have this right? The young

woman certainly didn't look like any maid that Jane had seen before. Yes, she wore a dark dress, but it was nicely made, not the sort of thing Jane would ever expect to see a white canvas apron tied around. Her fair hair was in a bun, just as Jane's was, but there the similarity ended. She had little ringlets framing her face. Not so many as a fine lady might have, but it certainly seemed a little inappropriate for a servant. To top it all off, she was straight-backed and had a very obvious confidence about her.

"Are you sure she's Miss Talbot's maid, Mrs Coleman?" Jane asked, her curiosity giving her the courage to speak.

"Then you see what I do, Jane! No better than she ought to be!" Mrs Coleman said for the third time, and Jane wondered idly for a moment at the origins of such a ridiculous expression.

No better than she ought to be. It made no sense whatsoever, even though Jane knew exactly what it was meant to convey. It was a phrase she'd heard more than once as she'd grown up in the orphanage, a phrase that was designed to suggest that a woman suffered lax morals or was even a little promiscuous. Just as Jane was about to silently declare Mrs Coleman to be mistaken, she watched as Emma Talbot's maid languidly reached out and took a shining red apple from the top of the box that Glyn Billington was carrying. The lad stood there simply looking at her, his mouth agape. The young woman was pretty enough, that was true, but not such a great beauty as to extract such an awe-laden response.

When the young woman bit into the apple, however, Jane felt her own mouth open. There was something provocative about it that she couldn't entirely explain, but there and then, she had a sense that Mrs Coleman might be right after all.

"Well, this won't get the house straight ready for the party, will it?" Mrs Coleman said with an uncustomary chuckle. "Right, Jane, I need you to check that all the guest bedrooms are fit and ready for tonight. I know they've already been done, but I don't want to chance it. I don't want one of the guests coming downstairs clutching a discarded polishing cloth like that dreadful vicar did last time!"

"Of course, Mrs Coleman," Jane said and darted away.

Jane crept about the upper corridors as silently as a

cat, popping into one room after the other and carefully scouring each for any signs of forgotten cleaning materials. In no time at all, she was walking into the last of the rooms, having found nothing untoward thus far.

The final room was to be no different, although Jane lingered for a few minutes. This was to be the room that Emma Talbot stayed in, and Jane found herself thinking about the well turned out maid. The young woman was a lady's maid, of course, for that was the only type of maid who travelled with her mistress for a simple overnight stay. Lady's maids were always a little smarter, it was true, but that young woman might have passed for lower-middle-class, had it not been for that slight air about her. Had Miss Emma Talbot not noticed it? Or was it perhaps not obvious, something which the young woman had never let her mistress see?

Jane realised she was a little fascinated with the maid, wishing that she could work for an employer who would allow her better clothes, nicer hair. She tried to imagine Mildred Collins' reaction if Jane were to attend to her duties with her soft brown hair turned into ringlets at the front. She winced and shook her head; such a thing would not be tolerated; she knew that without a doubt.

Jane sighed and wandered over to the window, peering out over the rooftops and chimneys which pierced the pale blue sky. Not for the first time, Jane found herself wishing that she worked for anybody else in London. But perhaps not *anybody* else; perhaps somebody like Miss Emma Talbot.

The truth was, Jane, wished that there was another way to live, but people of her class, particularly orphans with no family to rely upon, had little choice in the matter. The whole system relied upon the existence of the poor, for who else would look after the seemingly useless rich? Jane didn't want to look after the useless rich, and she certainly didn't want to look after Mr and Mrs Collins. At night, she dreamed of a better life. Imagining that she had wealthy parents who had simply misplaced her, who had lost her through no fault of their own and had no idea that she had been discovered and placed in an orphanage.

She'd never known anything about her family, about the circumstances which surrounded her appearance at the orphanage as a baby. She'd asked, of course, but nobody had ever told her anything. The guardians at the orphanage were hardly any kinder than Mildred Collins, and Jane had always been told, as had each and every one of the other children, that she had likely been abandoned by a mother of loose morals. One who had enjoyed all the benefits of marriage without ever having spoken her vows. None of the spite stopped her wishing that she'd known her parents; her mother. It was like a gaping hole at the very core of her that would never, ever be filled.

"Well, this won't get the house straight for the party, will it?" she said, quietly parroting Mrs Coleman's words.

With a sigh, Jane turned from the window and wandered back across the room, taking a final look around to be certain that nothing had been left behind before she left the room and closed the door behind her

CHAPTER TWO

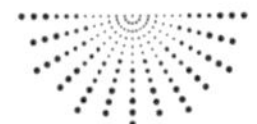

The day had passed quickly, the preparations leaving nobody a moment to spare for so much as a thought, never mind anything else. Mrs Coleman, always calm and efficient, remained so, even when forced to deal with her mistress' continual flapping and complaining. Although Jane felt nothing particularly warm for the unapproachable housekeeper, she couldn't help but admire her just a little.

With the food all taken up and set out on the buffet tables, Jane would have a little time to herself. She would not be needed again until the time came to start going up and down the stairs to bring down the empty platters and plates, the process of clearing away which would last late into the night.

"It's just bread and butter tonight, I'm afraid," Mrs Coleman said, nodding at what was left of the loaf on the table in the servants' dining room. "Help yourself, Jane, but just two slices, there are still one or two servants who haven't had anything yet."

"Yes, Mrs Coleman," Jane said and leaned over the table to cut herself two narrow slices which she buttered thinly. There was a jug of milk on the table, and she tipped a little into a mug before sitting down to enjoy the meagre meal.

Mrs Coleman hurried away, leaving Jane alone in the servants' dining room. She ate her bread-and-butter slowly, chewing thoughtfully as she wondered about her employers. All their guests seem to like them, and Jane thought it was likely because they seemed to be different people entirely in the company of others. They were open and smiling, friendly and warm, everything they were not to the people who worked for them.

"Dining alone?" The words were so well spoken that Jane almost got to her feet, thinking herself to be in the presence of one of the Collins' guests. However, when Miss Emma Talbot's maid wandered into the dining room, Jane stayed where she was. It was bad enough having to rise for the likes of Mildred and Rupert Collins, never mind clambering to her feet and bowing at other servants.

"Yes," Jane said, still a little awestruck even if the young woman was just a maid like her.

"Do you mind if I join you?" she went on, smiling and friendly with no hint of the sensual provocation she had lavished upon poor Glyn Billington. In fact, if Jane had not seen it with her own eyes, she would never have believed it.

"No, not at all," Jane said and felt a little shabby in this woman's presence.

"You're Jane, aren't you?" the woman continued in a light and friendly manner.

"Yes, I'm Jane. Jane Ashford."

"Well, I'm Maud Parsons, and I'm pleased to meet you," she said in her polite, cultured tones.

However, Jane was no fool, it was the sort of accent she'd heard before. More than one of the guardians at the orphanage had feigned a better station in life in just such a manner, and so Jane thought it unlikely that Maud Parsons was any better born than she was. Well, perhaps she hadn't been raised in an orphanage, but she certainly wasn't all she was pretending to be. Yet, despite all of that, Jane realised she was fascinated with Maud. There was something glamorous about her, even if she wasn't so very beautiful. There was perhaps even something exciting about her, something which might have made Jane a little envious if she wasn't quite so fascinated.

"It's nice to meet you too, Maud," Jane said, determined not to call her *Miss Parsons* and give her elevated status. "Have you worked for Miss Talbot for long?" she went on, conversationally.

"For five years now, Jane. I started working for her when I was no older than you are now," she said and smiled sweetly.

"Just five years and already you are a lady's maid?" Jane couldn't hide her admiration.

"Yes, I'm a lady's maid."

"You must have worked very hard to get such a

position." Jane really was impressed, and she realised that Maud could see it.

"I did work hard, but then everybody does, don't they? All of us in service work hard," she said, and Jane realised that she was beginning to like the young woman, regardless of the whole business with the apple and Mrs Coleman's assertion that she was *no better than she ought to be.* "No, I've been lucky too, and that's the truth."

"Lucky?" Jane knew she was prying a little, but she couldn't help it.

"Lucky to have a little bit of extra money here and there so that I could buy nice things. Like this dress, do you like it?"

"Yes, it's a very fine dress."

"If you have better clothes, you have a better chance of appealing to somebody like Miss Talbot. The younger women do like a lady's maid who is nicely turned out themselves. I suppose, looked at in a certain light that makes me something of an accessory. Like a pretty necklace or a hair comb with flowers in it."

"Don't you mind thinking about yourself in that way?" Jane asked and wished she hadn't, but Maud just laughed.

"No, not really. Let them think what they like, as long as they pay us properly." Her tone had become almost conspiratorial. Jane liked it, she bit her bottom lip and hoped for some advice.

"I wish mine did," she said in a whisper after looking over her shoulder to be sure they were alone. "Mr and Mrs Collins, I mean."

"A little on the mean side, are they?"

"They are very much on the mean side," Jane said and realised that she didn't feel an ounce of guilt; she felt no misplaced loyalty to Mr and Mrs Collins, that was the truth. She just needed her job, and that was all there was to it.

"It strikes me you need to find a better employer if you want to get on in this life," Maud said in a whisper. "Somebody who will pay you a little better so that you might have one or two nice things. If you have nice things, you have a better chance of getting the sort of position that you want."

"If I were to leave Mr and Mrs Collins, even in the spirit of goodwill, Mrs Collins might not necessarily provide me with a reference. She can be very awkward."

"Oh, yes, I know," Jane said, surprising her. "You must have seen it, Jane! Nobody likes her!" Maud began to laugh, a pretty, tinkling sound.

"The servants, you mean?"

"No, I mean all of them. Everybody. The upper classes are a funny set, Jane. They have everything they need, but they'll put up with anybody's company so that they might have a free meal. I suppose that's how they got rich in the first place, hanging onto everything they've got and taking everything they could. Mr and Mrs Collins put on a good spread, so everybody turns up. But nobody likes them. I know my mistress cannot abide them." Maud had leaned across the table and lowered her voice to something even less than a whisper, merely a mouthing of words.

Maud began to chuckle, and Jane followed suit. It was the first time she'd had a conversation in that house that she'd actually enjoyed; that she'd felt a real part of. It didn't matter to her now that Maud was *no better than she ought to be*, for Maud Parsons was actually noticing her, interested in her, even. It was something of a new and rather heady experience for a young orphan like Jane Ashford.

"Then you can see that I'm right; if it's inconvenient to Mrs Collins for me to leave, she certainly would withhold a reference, I know she would."

"I can imagine that is very true, my dear," Maud said and nodded thoughtfully. "I wonder if I could do anything to help." She chewed at the corner of her mouth and narrowed her eyes.

"You could? I mean, do you think so?" Jane asked and was unable to hide her excitement; could this be fate? Could this be fate throwing her into the path of somebody who might be able to help her out of the Collins' house?

"Let me think about it," Maud said and still looked thoughtful as she nodded slowly. "I think I might know just the person, and he's here tonight."

"He's here now?" Jane said, feeling excited and afraid. "But who is he?"

"Patience, Jane, I need to make an enquiry or two first. I don't want to go getting your hopes up if I'm mistaken... but I have an idea that I might be able to get you a better position as a housekeeper in a smaller establishment." Maud said in a breathy voice and was already getting to her feet.

Jane had hardly been able to concentrate the rest of the evening as she tried to imagine herself as a housekeeper. Surely, she was too young to be a housekeeper. But what did she know of the world? What did she know of life and work when she had only worked for Mr and Mrs Collins? Perhaps, in a smaller establishment, a housekeeper who was just thirteen and a half years old might be more normal than she imagined. And what did it matter if it was a smaller establishment if she was paid better and treated better? She wasn't the sort of servant who judged her own worth on the seeming wealth of her employer. The truth was, Jane didn't care who it was, as long as they treated her well.

When the time came to start collecting disused

plates and platters from upstairs, Jane's concentration hadn't improved any.

"Stack the platters, Jane, how many more times do I have to tell you?" Mrs Coleman said and stared at her intently. "What's the matter with you this evening? You're normally a little more alert than this."

"I'm sorry, Mrs Coleman," Jane said meekly, trying to snap out of it as she stacked silver platters in threes. She needed to concentrate; she couldn't risk anybody's suspicions, not even Mrs Coleman's.

"No matter, at least the guests have all retired to the drawing room. Some have even made their way to bed already. I'm not sure that's the mark of a fine party, although hand on heart, I know the food isn't to blame," Mrs Coleman went on as if speaking to herself. "I mean... look at it, hardly a thing left. And I had Cook make plenty too, hoping that we might get a little something ourselves at the end of it." She clicked her tongue disapprovingly.

"Shall I start taking these down, Mrs Coleman?" Jane asked, wanting to be on her own.

"Yes, I'll carry on stacking them, you start taking them down."

Jane walked smartly from the dining room, trying to give the impression of a maid who was concentrating, not one whose mind was filled with thoughts of escape. As she walked along the corridor towards the servants' staircase, a man stepped out in front of her, making her jump, and she almost let go of the platters.

"Steady on there, my dear girl," the man said and smiled broadly.

"I'm very sorry, sir," Jane said, knowing that the best thing was to always accept the blame when dealing with the upper classes; they expected it, right or wrong.

"Not at all, my dear, the blame is all mine. I'd wandered into the library for a little glance at Rupert's books before I went to bed. I was hoping to take something worth reading with me, but it appears they don't possess anything worth reading," he said, and his broad smile became something a little more mischievous.

Jane stifled a laugh, already deciding she liked this

particular guest. But then, hadn't Maud Parsons said that nobody particularly liked Mr and Mrs Collins? Still, there was something gratifying in witnessing it first-hand, she had to admit.

"It's all right to laugh, my dear. It's all right, I won't tell," he went on, and Jane finally gave in and laughed. "That's better; goodness, you are a pretty sort of thing when you laugh. I don't think I've ever seen you before, but it's no wonder. Mildred doesn't like young ladies who are prettier than she is, which of course, includes almost every young lady, it's true," he went on, continuing to berate his host and hostess. "But I can see why she keeps you out of sight when she has functions," he said.

"I... I... I only came up to clear away, sir," Jane said, feeling a little tongue-tied. There was something she liked about this man, something beyond his obvious dislike of the employers she disliked so terribly. He seemed fun, a little irreverent, and he had a nice face. He had dark hair and blue eyes, and he looked to be no more than twenty-seven or eight.

"Ah, then you must be Jane," he said, taking her off-guard. "You *are* Jane, aren't you?"

"Yes, sir, I am Jane. Jane Ashford."

"Well, Jane Ashford, I understand that you are in the market for a new employer if one can be found," he said and suddenly looked a little less mischievous and a little more intent. Jane immediately felt a flurry of panic; if this man knew that she was looking for greener pastures, surely it would only be a matter of time before others knew it too.

"Well... I..." Jane just didn't know what to say.

"Don't look so panicked, my dear. You have nothing to be afraid of, nothing at all. Unless, of course, you're afraid of coming to work in my house for more money and better conditions?" The mischief was back, his blue eyes wide and shining.

"Oh, I see," Jane said, realising that he must be the person Maud had imagined her working for. So, he was the employer with the smaller establishment who was looking for a housekeeper, was he?

"Well, what do you say? Are you to stay with Rupert and Mildred forever and put up with their less than generous terms, or are you to jump ship and come with me?" He seemed to want an answer immediately.

"If you have a position for me, sir, I would very gladly take it," she said, not giving herself time to think, not wanting to let this golden opportunity slip through her fingers.

"Then that is settled, Jane," he said and looked so pleased that Jane could hardly believe it. How long had he been looking for a housekeeper if he was this happy to have found one? "And don't worry, I'll square it all with Mildred. I'm sure she'll be a little terse with you for a few days, but then you'll be leaving, and you won't have to see that pasty face and that dreadful orange hair ever again," he said, whispering and pulling an amusing face.

Jane laughed; she couldn't help it. He was funny and a little cheeky, and she had no doubt whatsoever that life would be very different for her working in his house. She'd work hard, of course, she would, but she was certain she wouldn't feel that same sense of hopelessness, that same yearning for a life so very different. This was it; she was sure of it. Perhaps she didn't have wealthy parents who had simply misplaced her, but life was about to take a turn for the better, and Jane knew that she had Maud Parsons to thank for it all.

CHAPTER THREE

"Well, I shall be sorry to see you go, Jane," Mrs Coleman said in a surprisingly warm tone of voice. "You're the most efficient of the maids here, you'll do well," she went on, smiling. "But I can't say I blame you; a youngster like you working in a miserable place like this. No, I daresay things will be a little brighter working for that... What was his name again?"

"Mr Wakefield. Mr Franklin Wakefield." Just saying his name aloud filled Jane with excitement; it was the name which signified a new life, a new beginning, everything she had prayed for.

"That's it, Wakefield. He's not a regular guest here, that's why I keep forgetting his name. I reckon he's been here once or twice, but I'm not sure Mr and Mrs Collins like him very much." Mrs Coleman said, and Jane bit her tongue; she had been about to say that the feeling was mutual but thought better of It.

"I'm very grateful for everything you've taught me, Mrs Coleman," Jane said, feeling a little embarrassed but determined to say it, nonetheless. Mrs Coleman really had taught her a great deal.

"Well, you've listened, and you've tried hard, that's all a housekeeper could want out of a maid. And now you're to be a housekeeper yourself!"

"Not a housekeeper like you are, Mrs Coleman," Jane said, not wanting to appear too big for her boots. "As Maud said, Mr Wakefield has a very much smaller establishment than it is here. I don't expect he has so many servants."

"Yes, it looks like that Maud has done you a good turn. Mind you, I don't reckon I could have given in and trusted her the way you did." There was something in Mrs Coleman's words which, although Jane was sure she didn't mean anything by them, gave her a little frisson of caution.

"Do you think I was right to trust her?"

"She got you a good job, didn't she? No, I reckon I might have spoken a little too soon about that one. Mind you, if Mr Coleman was still alive, I wouldn't leave her alone with him for five minutes." She began to laugh, and so did Jane. "Have you got everything packed?" Mrs Coleman asked, changing conversational direction.

"Yes, although I suppose it's little enough," Jane said and shrugged. "I wonder what my room will be like when I get to Camden."

"It's hard to say, Jane. I mean, Camden is a far cry from Regents Park, isn't it? But I don't reckon that means a thing when it comes to what an employer is prepared to give. I mean, look at Mr and Mrs Collins," she went on and clicked her tongue. "This fine house in Regent's Park and not a moment's thought for the people who work for them. So, who's to say that a smaller house in Camden Town run by a better man might not provide better for you! Good luck to you, I say!"

Jane almost felt a little tearful at Mrs Coleman's words. Why was it on her very last day in that house that she had finally warmed to the housekeeper and, in turn, the housekeeper had finally warmed to her?

"Maud seemed to think that I would be better off, anyway. I mean, she must know something of Mr Wakefield to have been able to throw me into his path, so to speak."

"I don't doubt it," Mrs Coleman said, and Jane wondered if she was about to regurgitate the *no better than she ought to be* phrase. "It's good of him to come and collect you himself though, isn't it?"

"It is good of him; can you imagine Mr and Mrs Collins having collected me from the orphanage? I had to walk all the way from Southwark. Took me an hour, it did, carrying my little bag of things too. They could have just taken me with them there and then when they came out to choose a maid, but they just told me to get to their house the next day. Now that I know them better, I suppose it amused them to think of me walking all the way from the other side of the river." She shuddered at the thought of Mr and Mrs Collins, relieved to finally be away from them.

With any luck, she wouldn't set eyes on them again. At first, Mildred Collins had seemed pleased to be rid of her; so pleased, in fact, that she was almost pleasant. However, in the week that Jane had continued to work so that another maid might be found to take her place, Mrs Collins had returned to her old self, making barbed remarks about how she was no more likely to come up to Mr Wakefield's standards than hers. No, Jane wouldn't miss her one little bit.

"Well, I hear footsteps. Looks like your Mr Wakefield is going to collect you himself! I'll dare bet that's the first time he's ever approached the servants' entrance of a house!" Mrs Coleman said and laughed.

Jane suddenly felt nervous, her big hazel brown eyes wide as she looked up into Mrs Coleman's face. She realised that this was likely the last time she would ever see her, for she would certainly not be coming back to that house again. Camden Town was only a walk of a little over half an hour if she cut through Regent's Park, but Jane didn't imagine finding an excuse to visit. They were hardly friends, and she was certain Mrs Coleman wouldn't encourage such a thing. But suddenly, Mrs Coleman represented safety and stability, even in the midst of an establishment, Jane didn't particularly like. She suddenly wanted to cling to her, to throw her arms around her and beg her to say something to Mrs Collins so that she might stay. It was silly, she knew, for she would never be happy if she did stay. Deep down, Jane realised that Mrs Coleman, as harsh as she had been at times, had been as close as she had ever got to another person.

"I will miss you, Mrs Coleman," Jane said, blinking hard.

"Now then, none of that," Mrs Coleman said and patted her arm. "You don't want your new master seeing you all tearstained, do you? And you'll be fine, my dear. You're a good little maid, and you'll be a good little housekeeper, just remember that."

"Thank you, Mrs Coleman," Jane said, and hastily ran the corner of her shawl across her eyes to dry them.

"You look as if you've been crying, Jane," Franklin Wakefield said after they had travelled in silence for more than ten minutes.

He had indeed collected her from the servants' entrance himself, rather than leaving it to his driver.

He really was a most unusual man as far as Jane could tell. When he climbed into the carriage with her, sitting by her side rather than opposite, Jane had felt a little awkward. It was a far cry from the day that she had made her way to Regent's Park to work for Mildred and Rupert Collins, that was for certain. She couldn't imagine for a moment being allowed into the carriage, never mind having either one of them sit by her side for the journey.

"I'm sorry, Mr Wakefield. I was just a little sad to leave Mrs Coleman, that's all. I tried to tidy myself up, but you'd already arrived, sir."

"There's nothing to apologise for, as far as I can see," he said laughed, but it wasn't quite the easy and mischievous laugh of the previous week. He seemed apprehensive to her, and the very sense of it made her feel apprehensive herself. Was something different? "You seem to be a delicate flower, though. Perhaps you ought to be a little tougher for your own sake as much as anything else."

"Yes, sir," Jane said, and felt a little aggrieved; a child raised in an orphanage and sent into service at the age of twelve was tough enough, as far as she was concerned. She had lived a life that nobody in Mr

Wakefield's position would ever expect to, but now was not the time to think of such things.

Jane looked out of the window, surprised when she did not see the familiar sight of Regent's Park. Surely, they should have arrived in Camden Town by now, for it was far quicker by carriage than it was on foot. Jane had imagined that they would take the road which circled around the edge of the great park, only turning off as they neared Camden.

It wasn't that it didn't look familiar, because it did. In fact, Jane was almost certain that they were on the Tottenham Court Road; she recognised it from her journey on foot from Southwark eighteen months before. And were they not heading south rather than north? It didn't make sense. Camden Town was northeast of Regent's Park, not south of it. Surely, they were heading back towards the River Thames. Feeling suddenly disconcerted, Jane began to fidget in her seat.

"Is everything all right, Jane?" he asked, that apprehension in his blue eyes seeming to grow and grow.

"Yes," she said and knew that her voice had given her

away. "Well, no, sir. Surely, we're heading south towards the river, aren't we?"

"Yes, yes we are," he said, seeming a little as if he'd been caught out.

"But Camden is north, sir."

"It is, it is. And we shall be going there in a little while. For now, I have something to attend to, and I didn't think you would mind coming along with me."

"No sir, not at all," Jane said, hoping that her voice sounded amenable, for her senses were telling her that something was wrong. But what could be wrong? And why shouldn't he take her along on some errand if it made sense for him to do so? She was his employee now, the whole thing was up to him after all, wasn't it?

"You just relax, Jane. You just relax and don't worry about a single thing. You'll get used to my ways and, in the end, you'll realise just how much better off you are."

"Yes, sir," Jane said, the words, in the end, were somehow unsettling. *In the end*? But surely if she was better off, she would realise it immediately. *In the end?*

Jane looked out of the window again just as they began to cross the Waterloo Bridge. She looked out across the murky dark grey water of the River Thames and had the strangest sense of unwanted familiarity. This was the part of London she knew only too well and, if she didn't know better, she might think they were heading right back to Southwark.

But did she know better? She had no idea where they were going, and Franklin Wakefield certainly hadn't said. Perhaps the piece of business he had to conduct *was* in Southwark itself, although she could hardly imagine what. What on earth would a fine gentleman like Franklin Wakefield be doing in Southwark in the first place?

As the carriage took this road and then that, Jane had a creeping sense of unease. She recognised every street now, for they were surely not far from the orphanage in which she'd grown up. Her mouth began to go dry, even as she tried to tell herself that she was foolish for thinking she would ever be put back into the orphanage, not at her age. She was thirteen now, an age at which most orphans were already turned out of the dubious safety of the orphanage to find some work at the earliest opportunity or make their way directly to the workhouse. No, the orphanage would not be taking her back. Yet still, the sense of unease remained, and Jane realised that she had begun to feel a little afraid.

"Just relax, there's a good girl," Mr Wakefield said in a slow and smooth voice, reminding her of the way some of the street performers spoke; the ones who tried to convince everybody that they'd worked with the finest travelling circuses as hypnotists. She felt suddenly alert as if she needed to have every single one of her wits about her.

"Things always go better when we relax, my dear. That's right, just relax," he went on, his voice not at all soothing as he likely hoped, but rather sinister as he laid a hand on her shoulder.

Suddenly, he didn't seem quite so mischievous and fun anymore. He didn't seem young either, but rather a fully-grown man who well and truly held all the cards. Jane could feel her very insides trembling, and her stomach clenched, even though she did everything in her power not to show it.

"There's no need to be nervous, my dear. You'll get used to it."

"Get used to what?" she asked, unable to stop herself questioning her new employer.

"Be quiet now," he said as the carriage drew to a halt outside one of the worst taverns in Southwark. It was called the Dog and Duck, a name she had always thought ridiculous in such a grey and impoverished place.

Franklin Wakefield jumped down from the carriage, turning to help her. While she'd never travelled in a carriage before, she'd watched enough from the window in the Collins' home in Regent's Park to know that the driver ordinarily got down to help. This man, however, looked stoically ahead of him, almost as if he couldn't bear to turn his head and look down at her. Something about that made her feel even worse, and she had a sudden desire to run. However, just as the thought crossed her mind, Franklin Wakefield reached for her and took her firmly by the arm, leading her towards the battered wooden door of the tavern.

CHAPTER FOUR

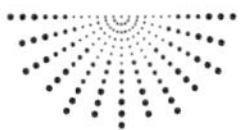

Still holding rather tightly to her arm, Franklin Wakefield walked the two of them awkwardly through the narrow doorway. Jane had never been inside a tavern before and wondered if they all smelled this bad.

The stench of sour ale seemed to rise up from the wooden floor to greet her, and the thick tobacco smoke made her cough. It was as if she had walked into a dense London fog, barely able to see for the heavy, acrid smoke which made the world suddenly appear sepia.

"I would prefer to wait in the carriage, sir. Surely you don't need me for..." she began, but Franklin squeezed her upper arm painfully. At that moment, at that very moment, Jane knew that she was in trouble.

"On the contrary, you're the very reason for my being here." Franklin's whole demeanour had changed into something she didn't recognise. No longer did his blue eyes look mischievous, rather they looked cold and cruel.

"I don't understand," Jane said, her heart beating so hard she could feel it in her throat.

"Come along," he said and drew her further into the dark, cave-like tavern.

They walked straight past the landlord, a fat man with a fulsome beard who smelled like rancid fish. He wore a grey waistcoat over a shirt which must surely have once been white, both garments liberally sprinkled with dubious stains. The landlord nodded at Franklin Wakefield before turning his attention to Jane, an ugly, lascivious smile spreading across his face.

Franklin continued to walk her through the tavern, pulling her through another doorway when she began to resist. They were at the bottom of a narrow staircase; she could see more clearly now that they were in place the smoke hadn't reached. As he drew her towards the staircase, she heard a shout from inside the tavern.

"That's the new one, is it? Who gets to go first?" It was a rough cockney accent, a grating, unforgiving accent.

"What? What did that man say?" Jane asked, and began to pull violently backwards, almost bent double as she tried to free herself.

"Maud thought you would be more open to this, my dear," Franklin said, holding onto her arm easily and smiling at her. How his face was changed now that she knew he was not a good man. She thought of Mrs Coleman and tears began to course down her cheeks.

"Open to what?" Jane shrieked, but she knew exactly what she had walked into. That dreadful rough voice peeling out from the other room had told her everything she needed to know about what was expected of her now. "What has this got to do with Maud? She told me that you needed a housekeeper, and so did you. That's what you said, sir. You said you needed a housekeeper!" She was yelling now, although she was certain that she could scream all she wanted, and it would do her no good.

"You wanted better, didn't you? You wanted fancy clothes and a few more coins in your purse, didn't you? Well, how on earth do you think a child like you might go about getting such things? Did you really think I would pay the earth for a housekeeper who had only ever been little better than a scullery maid? What do you know about running a house, little Miss Jane Ashford? Is it my fault that you didn't have the sense to see the offer I was truly making you?"

"Yes, yes, it is your fault. It is your fault for lying, for having me believe that I was going to be working for you."

"Believe me, Jane, you most certainly are going to be working for me. And you'll be working hard... if you know what's good for you," he said and winked at her, instantly turning himself from respectable gentlemen to guttersnipe.

"No, no, I won't. I want to go back to Regent's Park, and I want to go now," she said, twisting and turning to escape even as his thick fingers bit into the soft flesh of her upper arm.

"They won't have you back, Jane," he said and started to laugh, a low and cruel cackle. "I made sure of that."

"What?" Even as she asked the question, she knew that it was true. They would never have her back, not now. Mildred Collins would delight in turning her away, Jane knew she would.

"I made sure they knew that you were dissatisfied with them in every respect. I made sure that they knew you thought they paid paltry wages and behaved irrationally. I left them in no doubt whatsoever that you despise them to the very core of your being, my dear, for it does not suit my purposes to have you fleeing across the park and begging for sanctuary. If you want to survive now, if you want to eat and have a roof over your head, then it is to me you must turn. I own you now, Jane Ashford. And at the same time, I am your only saviour in this world. I am all that stands between you and the workhouse or the street, what do you say to that? Perhaps you think I'm clever? I know I do." He looked so self-satisfied that Jane knew, that had she been blessed with the strength of a man, she would have killed him with her bare hands there and then.

"I am just thirteen years old, sir," she said, deciding that she must appeal to his conscience... if he had one.

"That's plenty old enough. Do you think you will be the only one of your age making her living in this way?"

"I won't do it," Jane said defiantly, feeling like a fly caught in a spider's web as she tried harder and harder to free herself. But the harder she tried, the harder he held onto her, yet still, it didn't seem much of an effort for him. The sense of powerlessness made her both furious and terrified at the same time.

Suddenly, she found herself longing for the days of Mildred and Rupert Collins, their pernicious cruelty, their ugly satisfaction in tearing her down. She struggled, she closed her eyes and tried to bargain with the Lord; she would spend the rest of her life with Mildred and Rupert Collins and never, ever complain again. More than that, she would be thankful. She would be grateful to them. Anything but this; anything but this dreadful moment. If only she hadn't listened to Maud Parsons. If only she had silently denounced her that day that Mrs Coleman had said she was *no better than she ought to be*. Was this how Maud made enough money for nice things?

"Is this what Maud does?" Jane asked angrily; suddenly, she had to know.

"It's what she *did*, my dear. She fulfils another purpose for me now, a very important one. Perhaps you might fulfil that same purpose one day if you work hard enough as Maud did."

"What purpose?" Jane already knew the answer.

"Why, she finds girls like you, Jane. She finds them, she talks to them, she has them agree to come to me, and then they work for me. She was a very fine prostitute, and now she is a very fine procurer of others."

"A fine prostitute? There is no such thing!" Jane said, reacting violently to hearing the word said out loud. It was as if by giving voice to that one word, he had made it real. She kicked out at him, landing several blows on his shins with her booted foot. Once again, it seemed to make no difference.

"She was a fine prostitute because she did not resist it. Maud Parsons is a clever woman, and she was a clever girl. She understands the way the world works, and so she let it work. The more you let it work, the more it will work for you. One day you will thank me, Jane. One day you might have fine dresses and styled hair, perhaps you will even find yourself a position as a lady's maid as Maud did."

"But Maud worked for Miss Talbot for years, sir. That's how she worked her way up to being a lady's maid." Jane said and felt her heart sink when she heard his derisory laughter.

"Maud secured her position with Emma Talbot two years ago, that's all. And you want to know how? With the fine dresses she earned working for me, and with a reference cooked up by one of my dear friends. You see, I was right, wasn't I? Maud Parsons is a very clever woman."

Jane knew that Maud Parsons most certainly was a clever woman, but her intelligence was far outstripped by her deviousness. How she wished she'd never met her.

"I won't do this. Release me now, and I will go to the workhouse," Jane said defiantly, meeting his steely blue gaze without flinching.

"No, I don't think so. I've already gone to so much trouble, not least paying that ghastly Mildred a few pounds for you. No, it's time to get a return on my investment," he said, and without any warning whatsoever, he dipped forward and threw her over his shoulder, carrying her up the narrow staircase with ease.

Jane screamed all the way up the stairs, even though she knew it was to no avail. She felt sick as she pounded her small fists into Franklin Wakefield's back, having no more effect on him than if she'd been a fly buzzing about his face. He walked along a narrow corridor before kicking open a door and carrying her into a small room, carelessly banging her head against the door frame as he went. She cried out, but he just tutted and threw her down onto the bed.

Jane would have prayed for deliverance if she could clear her mind of fear for long enough to do so, but she couldn't. She could hear heavy footsteps on the stair treads, somebody was coming. In her heart of hearts, she knew it wasn't somebody coming to save her unless the driver who could not bear to look her way had finally found a conscience somewhere in his body. She doubted it and, of course, she was right. When the landlord of the pub appeared in the doorway, his ugly smile more lascivious than it had been downstairs, she realised that he was to be the first to sample the new merchandise.

"Same terms as usual?" the landlord said to Franklin, both of them were ignoring the crying girl on the bed.

"Yes, of course. Always free to my host, Jack!" Franklin said, and the two men burst out laughing. It was hideous, appalling, two grown men making a joke at her expense, not caring that she was terrified and already humiliated before the worst of it had even begun.

Franklin retreated from the room, but not far. Jane heard him take just a few steps and then stop. Just a few feet away, and with the door left wide open, she knew he would be listening. What a vile, sick creature he was.

The room smelled bad enough already, but the stench coming from the landlord was beginning to swell and mix with the bad air, making it almost impossible for her to breathe. Added to the smell of rancid fish was the stink of whiskey, almost as if he had drunk so much of the stuff that it seeped out through the pores of his skin. He paused just a few feet from the bed and began to unbuckle the battered old leather belt holding up his filthy trousers. He swayed a little, seemingly unable to keep his balance as he looked downward.

Jane backed away, scampering up the bed until she collided with the headboard. She knew it didn't matter how far she scampered, how much she recoiled, this dreadful, disgusting man was going to do exactly what he wanted with her and there was nothing she could do about it. There was no escape, not with him standing between her and the door.

"I reckon I'd be the first, wouldn't I?" the landlord said in a rough, deep voice. "I always like it when Mr Wakefield finds me a nice fresh one." His words were slurred, and she knew he was drunk. If only he had taken just one more drink and collapsed in a heap. "Them downstairs, they won't care that I was the first to have you. They're the dregs, they are, take what they're given, they would," he went on, his voice taking on a pompous aspect as if he really was a man of note.

"How can you do this? How can you treat me this way? What God do you pray to that you think this is all right?" she cried, desperately trying to put off the inevitable.

"I don't pray to any God, you silly girl. Why would I bother to pray to a God who's never done nothing for me, eh?"

"I was raised in an orphanage, but that doesn't mean I just turn my back on God and do whatever I want, does it? I hope you go to hell for this. I hope you go to hell and roast for all eternity. I hope you suffer as you mean to make me suffer, you foul, disgusting pig!" Jane was angry now, no longer believing that appeasement of any kind would work in her favour. She was about to be defiled, and she would say whatever she liked. She hated this man, and she wanted him to know it. She wanted him to know exactly how low she thought him, no matter that he wouldn't care one way or the other. Her anger was leading her now, and it was the strangest feeling.

"I don't care what you think of me. All I care about

now is that you're going to make me feel good; why would I care about anything else? Just shut up and do as you're told. Just shut up and do your job, earn your living, you worthless prostitute," he said and grinned, enjoying himself, finding his insult a pleasure.

"I am not a prostitute, and I will never, ever be a prostitute," Jane said in a low voice, that anger making her feel curiously alive and vile all at once. She knew she had to do something; the anger was demanding action. The anger was demanding that she didn't just sit there and give up without a fight.

Still struggling with his belt buckle, the fat landlord looked down again and, just as before, she could see him wobbling precariously. Now was her moment to act.

She knew she couldn't be saved, not now, but at least her anger, her fight, would always let her know that she had struck back. So, without wasting a moment, she got up from the bed and flew towards him, shoving him hard in the chest as he still looked down at his belt buckle. The man toppled immediately, his drunkenness an ally to her. He fell back to the floor, landing hard on his backside. She didn't wait to see how he fared, how long it would take him to get up, she just ran for her life.

Everything had happened so fast that Franklin Wakefield was still standing at the top of the stairs by the time she flew down the corridor. He looked at her with such surprise that she almost laughed, even though she knew that she was sunk now, this was it. He would grab her and drag her back into that bedroom, despite the anger which still powered her.

However, the anger had other ideas. The anger took over completely, taking away her pain, her thoughts, her planning. Without a single thought to guide her, Jane simply ran towards Franklin, her fury coming from her in a deep, guttural cry as she pushed hard at his chest with both hands, throwing all of her tiny weight behind it and toppling him, just as she had toppled the landlord. However, when Franklin fell, he did not land on his backside. Instead, he flew backwards down the stairs, the sound a terrible rumble which shook her out of her trancelike state and back into the reality that was hers.

Now that the anger had subsided, fear was her new driver. Self-preservation gripped her, and she ran down the stairs. She paused only briefly as she neared the bottom, for Franklin Wakefield's body was a crumpled heap, his legs still on the stairs, his torso, arms, and head, sprawled awkwardly on the flagstone floor.

With barely a pause, Jane leapt across him, landing awkwardly on the other side of his body, and almost losing her footing. She righted herself and continued to run. She burst through the door that he had dragged her through just minutes before and tore through the smoky Tavern, the dense sepia world was suddenly her friend. The drunken, useless men in that room hardly had room for an independent thought, never mind quickly working out what had happened and stopping her from escaping. Weaving through them, she burst out of the small battered wooden door into the street beyond, dragging in her first breath of clean air as if her life depended on it. She ran, racing past the carriage, the driver turning to look at her.

"Look at me now, would you? You shameful creature!" she said, stopping dead in her tracks and yelling at him, her voice raw and her eyes wide and accusing.

The driver stared at her, a mixture of shame and

guilt on his face. If she wasn't so afraid, she might even have felt a little sorry for him.

"Run!" he said, his eyes darting towards the door she had just flown out of. "Run, for God's sake!" he said, and she did just that.

She couldn't let them catch her; she couldn't be dragged back into that place. She had just killed a man; she knew it wouldn't go well for her. She was just an orphan with nobody to care for her, nobody to believe her. Those men could tell any lie they liked; the peelers would believe them. They were all men; they were all the same. Even one who seemed to have a capacity for shame like the driver would easily turn his back, wouldn't he? And he had, hadn't he? So why on earth would Jane ever believe that any man on God's earth could be any different?

Jane ran and ran with no idea of where she was going. She ran knowing she had nobody to run to. She ran non-stop for almost a mile turning down alleys, hoping to put off anybody who might be running behind her. She ran until she tripped over something and was sent sprawling facedown onto the cold grey cobblestones.

CHAPTER FIVE

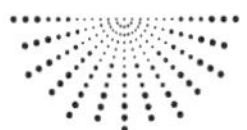

"Oi!! What are you doing? You could have squashed me flat as a pancake!" came a very young but very persistent voice. "You all right?" The voice became suddenly caring, switching instantly in the way that only a small child's could. "Oh, my Gawd, are you dead, Miss?"

Jane couldn't respond. She'd hit the ground hard, and every inch of air had been forced from her lungs in a terrible gust. She was fighting to draw a breath in now, but it wouldn't come. It was as if she'd forgotten how to breathe. Jane wondered if this was the end. Perhaps it would be for the best. She could die here and now and know she had at least won the last of life's battles. She had escaped without being violated. She could die peacefully.

"Aren't you going to speak? Your eyes are open, you can't be dead, can you?" The little voice had moved, and now Jane could see its owner; a tiny girl of no more than six years old; thin, short, and covered in dirt.

Jane closed her eyes, preparing to move into the world beyond when a great shriek made her eyes fly wide open again. When her windpipe burned, she realised the shriek was hers. She might have given up on life at that moment, but her body hadn't. Finally, it had clawed at life, dragging air into her body at speed. Her throat was raw and aching, her chest tight and feeling bruised.

"Gawd, what's wrong with you?" the little girl asked, staring at Jane with open curiosity as if the circus was in town and she'd managed to sneak her way into the big top. "What was that 'orrible noise?" She peered closer still as Jane, breathless, tried to get up.

"I'm sorry," Jane said as she got to her feet. "I didn't mean to run into you. I was just..." She paused; she didn't know what to say.

"You was just running away from someone, weren't you?" the girl said and shrugged as if running away from someone was just one of life's many ordinary pastimes.

"I need to keep going," Jane said, holding her ribs as she looked behind her. She couldn't hear anyone following, but she was terrified of being captured. She had to keep moving.

"Peelers, is it? What did you do?" The little girl was grinning, seemingly impressed. Something about it annoyed Jane, and she wanted to shock the child.

"I just killed a man!" Jane said and looked at the little face viciously.

"Then you need somewhere to hide, Miss," the child said in such a matter of fact way that Jane felt guilty for her spite; what had happened to this tiny girl that she wasn't shocked by a declaration of murder?

"Yes, I do. Do you know somewhere I can hide?" Jane smiled as best she could; she needed to win the girl over, not make her afraid.

"Come on," the girl said and set off fast, leaving Jane to limp along behind her as best she could.

They turned up and down so many alleyways that Jane knew she would never find her way back alone. She felt vulnerable again, a sense of doom overwhelming her, but she knew she had no choice. Whatever lay ahead of her, for good or bad, was unavoidable now. So, she followed, trusting her life in the hands of a tiny street urchin.

"In 'ere!" the girl said, disappearing down some stone steps at the side of a derelict row of terraced houses. "In the basement. The peelers always look for people hiding upstairs in these abandoned places. They're too stupid to imagine we'd live in the basement like servants when we might have the whole ruined house to ourselves. That's what Harry says, anyway!"

"Harry?" Jane said, immediately afraid; another man, was it? Another man with just his own best interests at heart?

"Come on! Quick! We don't want anyone to see us dipping down here!" The girl reached back for Jane's hand, and she took it.

The two girls went in through the door which the little one was careful to close behind them. Jane stood as still as a statue for a moment, feeling suddenly blind in the gloom. She blinked rapidly as she tried to get her bearings, seeing a pale-yellow glow in the distance. The little girl, clearly accustomed to her surroundings, darted away through the darkness, leaving Jane there alone.

Feeling afraid, pinning all her hopes for survival on a tiny child, Jane set off after her. She called out, the panic clear in her voice until the little girl came back for her.

"What's the matter?" the girl said in confusion.

"I can't see where I'm going," Jane said, feeling close to tears. It was cold and damp and so dark she felt as if she were in her own grave.

"Don't worry, you'll get used to it," the girl said, that tone of caring in her young voice enough to make Jane's tears spill over.

"What's your name?" Jane asked, trying to divert the girl's attention as she surreptitiously dragged the corner of her woollen shawl across her eyes to dry them.

"I'm Sally. What's your name?"

"I'm Jane," Jane said, and felt relieved as her eyes adjusted to the gloom and little Sally came into focus.

"Pleased to make your acquaintance," Sally said in a humorous imitation of an upper-class accent. Despite herself, Jane laughed, and Sally seemed delighted by it.

"What is this place?"

"It's where we live," Sally said, her child's blunt confusion summed up in a shrug.

"And who is we? Who lives here with you? Your parents?"

"Parents? I never had no mother or father, Jane." Sally laughed as if it ought to have been obvious.

"Neither have I," Jane said and reached out to ruffle the child's filthy hair.

"You ain't no street kid, Jane. You don't speak like a street kid," Sally said, sheepishly, as if it were an insult.

"I was in the orphanage in Southwark."

"We are in Southwark. Surely, you ain't running

away from the orphanage, it's just streets away from here; are you?" There was a harshness to Sally's laugh.

"No, I'm not."

"You didn't kill one of the guardians, did you?" Sally laughed all the harder.

"No, I didn't. It wasn't a guardian; it was a very bad man who was trying to hurt me."

"How comes you speak like that? I mean you're not posh, not exactly, but you're not exactly one of us either," the child said, full of curiosity again.

"I worked in service at a house in Regent's Park. The housekeeper tried to teach us all to speak a little better because it annoyed the mistress when we didn't. I suppose it's just stuck."

"It sounds funny, you sounding the way you do but not looking posh. It's like you ain't fish and you ain't fowl." Sally shrugged again, probably not realising the truth of her childish statement. Jane really was neither fish nor fowl; she didn't fit anywhere.

She wasn't a street child, but neither was she the same girl who'd been taken from the orphanage. And she wasn't the sort of girl who would be able to turn up at a fine house and expect work anymore. For one thing, she had nothing but the clothes she stood up in, and in just a few days and nights in such surroundings, as she found herself now, she would look rough. She had left everything behind in Franklin Wakefield's carriage, and it was little enough as it was. But little enough was better than nothing, wasn't it?

"Come on, let's keep moving," Sally said and took her hand again.

She led her through the low, cold rooms of the basement until they ended up at the light Jane had been able to see in the distance.

As her surroundings became clearer, Jane realised she was looking at a cluster of little faces. Children the same age, or similar, to Sally; boys and girls, all ragged, all dirty. They looked up at her from where they sat on the floor on old rugs and blankets. There were two oil lamps and what looked like wooden packing boxes everywhere. Jane smiled at the children, wondering who there was in the world to look after them. They were so tiny, so thin, and so very dirty.

"Hello," Jane said, her softly spoken voice like a shout in the silence. She looked at the tiny faces, counting seven children in all if she included Sally. "Do you live here by yourselves?" she went on, wondering why they didn't speak.

She let her eyes stray to the wooden crates and realised that, on the top of each stack, there were metal cages. Wire crates, battered and twisted. In the pale light, she peered hard into one of the cages, her eyes fixed on little lights inside. In a heartbeat, she realised that the little lights were simply the reflection of the oil lamps in so many tiny eyes. She could see movement in the crates now, black mounds tumbling over each other, creating a scratching sound that made the hair on the back of her neck stand up.

At the moment that she realised they were rats, at the moment that she opened her mouth to scream, a hand clamped down hard over her lips, an arm seizing her roughly around the waist from behind.

"No, they don't live here by themselves."

CHAPTER SIX

"Now then, we don't have no screaming down here, do you understand? Now, I ain't gonna hurt you, none of that, I just don't want to let you go until I'm sure you're not going to yell your bleeding head off," the voice was raspy, rough, and the grip upon her every bit as firm as Franklin Wakefield's had been.

"Mmmm," she said, unable to produce any other sound.

"What was that? Was that you telling me you won't scream when I let go of you?" he asked, and Jane nodded furiously, her head constricted somewhat by the grip on her face.

"Because if you do, then I *will* hurt you, do you understand?"

"Mmmm." She made the same noise again and tried to nod her head even more firmly.

Finally, the man let go of her and Jane turned sharply round to look at him. He wasn't very much taller than her, but he was stocky. He was unkempt, but nowhere near as unkempt as the children seemingly in his care. How could the man look stocky when the children looked so thin? Was he really looking after them, or was something else going on here? Despite having grown up within the confines of the orphanage, Jane knew enough of the area to know that it was a perfect portrait of the cruelty of London. Poverty and unfairness made even the impoverished unfair. This was dog eat dog, and she was fairly certain that this man was a wolf.

"Who are you?" Jane asked, surprised that her voice sounded steady even though she was so desperately afraid.

"Now, you're the one who's wandered into my patch, girl, so I'll be the one who asks the questions," he said and gave a chuckle that was almost friendly. "Who are you?" he went on.

"Jane, Jane Ashford."

"So, Jane Ashford, what brings you down here to see me?" He laughed again. "Apart from Sally, that is." Jane turned to look at Sally, wondering if she was simply a smaller, younger version of the self-serving Maud Parsons. But Sally looked up at her with an encouraging smile, dissolving her suspicion.

"I needed somewhere to go, and Sally led me here," Jane said, not wanting to tell him everything.

"She was running from the peelers, Harry," Sally said and smiled at Jane, clearly thinking that she was being helpful.

"It wasn't the peelers, I was just..." Jane said, not wanting this man to know everything about her.

"Who were you running from?" Harry said and ran his hand through a thick, dry beard which made a rasping noise as he did so.

"She was running because she killed a man," Sally went on, innocently giving Jane away. "It's all right,

Harry, he was a bad man, and he was trying to hurt her."

"Is that so?" Harry tipped his head to one side as if expecting more information from Jane. "So, who was it that you killed?"

"It doesn't matter, it was an accident. The man was trying to hurt me and it just..."

"Who?" Harry said, the sudden shout making the children jump a little in surprise.

"He would have..."

"Jane Ashford, if you don't tell me right now who you killed, I'll march you straight down to the peelers until they find out which man lays dead within a mile from here. And then guess what? It will be the gallows for you, so you'd be better off telling me, wouldn't you?" He chuckled again, but it was a far less friendly sound than it had been before.

"His name was Franklin Wakefield," Jane said, her voice sounding like a sigh of resignation; now this man had a hold on her. Now this man had everything he needed to turn her in, and all that remained now was for her to wait and wonder what she would have to do to spare her own neck. She had jumped out of the frying pan and run straight into the fire.

"Oh, I see," Harry said and shrugged nonchalantly. "Well, I'm Harry, as you probably already guessed. Harry Newland, at your service," he said in that strange imitation of a refined accent, just as Sally had done earlier. He held out his hand and Jane, still shaking, took it.

"And you live here?" Jane asked tremulously, not knowing if she was yet allowed to ask questions.

"We all live here, Jane. And you live here too, don't you?" It was a question, but Jane sensed that she would only be able to give one answer; yes.

"Well, I..."

"Of course, you live here. It's better than nothing, isn't it? It's certainly better than the workhouse. More importantly, it's a lot better than swinging by your neck with your little feet kicking ten to the dozen whilst you try to free yourself from the noose," he said in such a matter-of-fact voice that his words, already gruesome, sounded so much more frightening than they would have done had they have been delivered in a more threatening tone. The hair on the back of her neck was standing up again, reminding her of the moment she had realised she was staring at cages full of rats.

Just as she thought of the rats, she suddenly became aware of the constant scratching and squeaking, the rummaging and rattling in the cages. Why hadn't she noticed it before? Had fear made her deaf? But now that she had noticed it, now that she had allowed the sound into her consciousness, she had a terrible feeling that it would never, ever end. They would scratch and squeak perpetually until she couldn't bear it any longer and she ran up the steps to the gallows as a means of escape from it all.

"Why do you keep rats?" Jane asked, wrapping her arms around herself and shuddering. "Surely, you would want to keep them out of here, not invite them in," she went on, not wanting to talk about her reasons for being there any longer; not wanting to hear another thing about how she would hang if she gave Harry Newland any reason to give her away.

"Because them little beasties in there, Jane, they're gold."

"Gold?"

"Well, not gold exactly, but *coin* nonetheless."

"You make money out of rats?" Jane said, but her confusion began to clear. "You're a rat catcher?"

"I'm not only a rat catcher, girl, but the reason the rats need removing in the first place. That's why I keeps 'em, you see?" He raised his eyebrows at her and looked pleased with himself, almost proud. "You look confused, let me help you with that," he went on and laughed. "Everybody here works, you see. Nothing in this life is free after all, is it? I'm not running a bleeding orphanage."

"Works?" Jane said, remembering how Franklin had told her she would be working hard for her living.

"That's right, that's why they're all so thin. I need them that way, you see. I need them to be able to sneak in places, crawling through the slimmest gap in an open sash window. Just those little gaps that people think are safe enough to let the air in. But they're letting in more than the air, aren't they? They're letting in my clever plan, my fine little workers and their precious cargo."

"Cargo?" Jane said, and he laughed at her confusion.

"My little girls and boys here are the ones who carry the rats into these fine houses in the first place. They're small and quick, they are, I've never had one of them caught yet. They sneaks in through any gap they can find, carrying a little bag of my shining black beauties with them, ready to set them free before they hurry away into the night."

"You put rats into people's homes just so that you can catch them?"

"Catch them and be paid for my trouble, Jane. It's a good plan, isn't it?" Harry Newland spoke with confidence, not bothering to hide his devious game from her. But why would he? Why would he fear her going to the authorities when he already had enough information about her to send her to the gallows? Of course, he was confident.

"Yes, it's a good plan," Jane said, utterly disgusted by the dishonesty of it all but knowing that Harry Newland represented her only chance for survival. She couldn't go against him; she had to agree with every word he said.

"And better still, if one of my rats produces a ton of

babies. They're the most grateful, Jane, them that's being overrun with the little devils." He laughed heartily, thoroughly enjoying himself.

"Don't you worry about the children?" Jane asked, looking down at the dirty, innocent little faces and feeling that her heart might break.

They were like her, in their own way. They were lost in this world with nobody else to turn to, nobody to care for them. They were at his mercy just as she was at his mercy and, if it hadn't been him, it would have been some other man wanting some other thing. Perhaps there was some comfort that it was just rats, not something worse. Not the very thing that she had been expected to do by Franklin Wakefield. But this was London, and justice was swift and without mercy. If any of these children were caught, they would be punished, no doubt about it. They might not yet go to the gallows, but they would certainly be incarcerated or forced into the workhouse. Wasn't it all the same thing? Wasn't every option just as bleak as its nearest neighbour?

"I trained them well, Jane. I've given them every bit of knowledge I've got to give, so if they get caught, it's their own bleeding fault for not listening to me in the first place."

"They're so thin," she said, knowing that she ought to stop speaking, but she was unable to.

"I said to you before, I needs them thin, don't I? I need them small enough to get in through the little gaps in the dead of night. Thin and fearless, that's what these little ones are!" He turned to smile at the children, their little faces peering back at him.

He looked proud of them, almost like a parent, and it was the most curious experience. He was cruel, no doubt about it, but he had a way with him; a way which likely convinced these poor little scraps that he cared for them. It sickened Jane to the very core of her being, but she knew she must fight to hide that disgust.

"Don't look like that, Jane Ashford!" he said, narrowing his eyes and taking a step towards her. "That's right, you needn't look so hoity-toity about the whole thing. It's not like I don't feed them, is it?" He opened his tatty thick black coat and reached into the pocket on the inside. He pulled out a loaf of bread, the children suddenly starting to fidget with excitement as he did so. "I look after them good enough, girl. I put a roof over their heads and food in their bellies, and I keeps them safe. This is how the world works, and you'd better get used to it."

It was the second time that day that Jane had been told by an ugly, selfish man that *this was how the world worked.* She watched as he broke the bread into pieces with his filthy hands, handing each chunk to one child after another. They didn't mind his filthy hands; they were just so hungry. Jane looked at them as they tore into the bread, barely chewing before they swallowed down great mouthfuls of it. There was no enjoyment in the food, just a human being's instinct for survival. She could feel tears welling hot in her eyes as she looked at them, and she wondered how it was that such things were allowed to happen. If this was *the way the world worked*, it wasn't their fault, was it? It was the adults, the men and women, they had decided how things would be. Even those who didn't decide it allowed it, didn't they? People like that driver, turning their eyes away from what they didn't want to see. Protecting their own hearts from what they didn't want to feel.

Well, Jane would never be one of them. She would never turn her eyes away or harden her heart to such sights. She would feel every ounce of it, the sorrow, the pain, the heartbreak; she was a human being, and she would always be so. She would never become one of the hordes who determinedly denied to themselves that such things happened. And so, Jane let her tears fall, rolling down her cheeks unchecked.

She didn't care if the rat catcher saw her tears, she would have him know that she was a human, a real human. In the end, he did look at her, tilting his head to one side in what she was realising was a habit of his. A smile slowly made its way across his face as he looked at her. It was a mocking smile.

"Oh, dear, you're one of them that lets her heart bleed, aren't you? Well, you stick with Harry, girl. You stick with Harry, and you let him teach you how to let go of the fine thoughts and the fine feelings. If you don't, you'll suffer through every part of this life. It doesn't do to be so soft in the middle as you seem to be. You'll get taken advantage of if you don't learn to be different."

His tone of voice suggested kindly advice, but it was the advice of the hypocritical sort. She was being advised that people would take advantage of her by a man who clearly had every intention of doing just that.

This was, without a shadow of a doubt, the very worst day of Jane's life. It seemed like years ago that she had said goodbye to Mrs Coleman. It seemed like another life, and yet it was only that morning. In a few short hours, Jane had become a murderess; a girl on the run; a girl at the mercy of the rat catcher.

CHAPTER SEVEN

Jane slept fitfully, finding the bare floor with just a blanket over it hard and painful. Despite the deprivations of her life, she had always had something to sleep on. In the orphanage, she'd had a tiny mattress in a large room filled with tiny mattresses. At the Collins' house in Regent's Park, she'd had a bed. It was a small, iron-framed bed with a lumpy mattress on top of it in a room that was all her own. It had been her only joy in that house, to have a room to herself. For a year and a half, Jane had enjoyed absolute privacy at night. If only she'd had the sense to be grateful for that and stay right where she was.

Now, everything had been taken from her; the

mattress, the privacy, and any sense of tentative security she might have felt before. She was utterly exhausted, but she couldn't sleep for more than a few minutes at a time. Every time her eyes closed, and she felt herself drifting, she heard the scratching of the rats and her eyes flew open again. Whenever she settled herself about the rats, reminding herself that they were in cages, a horribly clear image of Franklin Wakefield lying twisted at the bottom of the stairs in the Dog and Duck Tavern assaulted her, once even making her cry out.

Every time she woke, she looked around her at the tiny bodies under the ragged blankets laying on the floor all around her. They didn't stir, and she wondered how it was that they slept so peacefully. Perhaps they didn't know any different from this. Perhaps they had never known anything better.

Harry Newland had told her that she might stay the night, but she knew deep down that she would be there for so much longer. He'd already told her that she lived there now, contradicting himself. However, Jane had the idea that he had contradicted himself intentionally, keeping her alert and uncertain of the world around her. Making it easier for him to control her. She didn't have much experience in the world, but she could see right through Harry as if he were a pane of glass.

In the orphanage, Jane had become a very good judge of character. Not of the children around her, her fellow orphans, but of those who called themselves guardians. She saw how they used praise as a means of drawing the children in, making them work harder, and then how they retracted that praise to deflate and defeat. It was all manipulation, every bit of it. As far as Jane could tell, that was what the world of fully-grown men and women was all about. Manipulation; getting every ounce you could get out of another human being. Apparently, that was *the way the world worked.*

Mildred and Rupert Collins had given her a fair insight into recreational cruelty. They were never violent, they never lashed out, they were just sarcastic and spiteful. Always taking the upper hand that life had given them at birth. They delighted in the poverty of those who could do no more in this world than find work looking after *them*. It had taken her a little while, but Jane had got the measure of them in the end. They were sad creatures who could only find their pleasure outside of themselves, and that pleasure could only be derived from belittling others.

Then there was Maud Parsons, closer in nature to Harry Newland than she would have cared to hear about. From a poor background, she had decided to help the more privileged use and manipulate her own kind and for her own purposes. Just like the rat catcher, she had no feelings of empathy for those whose start in life had been so similar to her own.

Franklin Wakefield hardly needed a description of any kind; a liar and a cheat who clearly maintained his lifestyle by setting young women and girls to work in the vilest profession imaginable. Jane wished she'd been able to see through him as she had seen through so many others.

It was sad, but the closest thing to a decent human being she'd met thus far had been Mrs Coleman, and even she had withheld her meagre warmth until the very end.

And then there was Jane Ashford herself; did she need any more words to describe her than just one? Murderess. But murderess that she was—did she really deserve to hang for her crime? She knew in her heart that she would never have committed such an act if Franklin hadn't taken her to that dreadful tavern in the first place. If she hadn't been trying to save herself, she would never have thought of pushing him, and certainly not when he stood at the top of a flight of stairs.

Unbelievably, she had encountered each and every one of those people in that one fateful day. She had spent her time with them all, one after the other, finally ending up becoming one of them. A woman who had done something which had shamed and changed her. She had killed another human being. More unbelievably still, her repetitive thoughts finally lolled her to sleep. She had slept a little longer this time, she was sure of it when the sound of movement drew her sharply awake.

She sat bolt upright, ready to protect herself. By the weak light thrown out by just one oil lamp, Jane could see that all the children were moving, getting themselves up out of their makeshift beds as if ready to start their day. But surely it was still the middle of the night, wasn't it? Jane looked around in confusion.

"It's time for them to go to work, Jane. No sense

sending them out in broad daylight with a bag of rats now, is there?" Harry said and chuckled.

Jane got to her feet and started backing away the moment that Harry opened the first of the cages and reached in for a rat. Expertly, he caught it by the tail and pulled it clear of the cage. He dropped it headfirst into a small cotton canvas sack, clamping the fabric closed in his fist as he reached into the cage for another rodent.

The rats were large, clearly better fed in their own way than these tiny children were, but still, he put them four to a sack. He tied a string around the top of each small sack and set them on the floor, and Jane could feel her stomach begin to heave as she watched the sacks moving, alive with rats.

"All right, you all know where you've got to go now, don't you?" he said, and the children nodded as one.

"Work in pairs as always. One of you goes in, the other one stands outside on watch. If any of you gets caught, the rest of you just run. But you just make sure there ain't no peelers behind you before you run all the way back here, do you understand?" He sounded gruff now, using his anger on exhausted, sleepy children, gaining full control. Once again, they all nodded meekly.

Harry bent down and picked up the first sack, handing it to a small boy. The boy took it. No sign on his pale but dirty face showed that he was repulsed. There was no sign that he felt anything at all. He simply took the sack in both hands, so little that four large rats were heavy for him.

Harry picked up the remaining two sacks handing one to another little boy, the other to a girl. The children began to walk away, heading out into the dead of night without the need for any further instruction. Little Sally brought up the rear, and Jane realised then that she was in charge. She was in charge of the children who were going out to set rats free in fine homes. Sally was Harry Newland's second-in-command.

"Keep your eye on them, Sally. And mind you don't let any of them run back here if there's peelers giving chase. That's the most important bit of the lot, do you hear me?"

"Yes, Harry," Sally said in her little girl voice.

As the children disappeared out into the night, Jane

stood with her arms wrapped around her, her fears bubbling up once more.

"Why do you stand like that, Jane? Why are you holding on to yourself for dear life?" Harry asked, eyeing her keenly.

"My ribs hurt," she said, telling the partial truth. Her ribs really did hurt, she was lucky not to have broken them when she'd tripped over Sally and landed so hard on the ground. However, it was her fear coming at her again, her instincts telling her that Harry was not a man to be trusted.

"Your ribs?"

"I tripped over Sally when I was running."

"When you were running away, you mean," he said and scratched his beard, making more noise than the remaining rats in their cages. "So, somebody had called the peelers then?"

"I don't know."

"Who were you running from then if it wasn't the peelers? This Franklin Wakefield's men, was it?"

"I don't know."

"How can you not know who was chasing you?

"I'm not even sure that anybody *was* chasing me, I just ran."

"How did you kill 'im?"

"Does it matter? He's still dead, isn't he?" Jane said, regretting her sharp tone the moment she saw his face change. He looked annoyed, a poor man's version of haughty. "I'm sorry. I'm still very shaken. I didn't mean to kill him, I just had to get away."

"So, what did he do to you?" His face had softened, and she wondered, for a moment, if what she could see in his dark eyes was genuine interest.

"He offered me a job, Harry, a position in his household. I worked for a family in Regent's Park, and I'd been there for more than a year. They were miserable people, and I was desperate to get away from them. I just wish I'd known that there were worse people than them in the world before I set off this morning."

"Beat you, did they?" he asked, almost conversationally as he sat himself down again and wrapped one of the ragged blankets around him. He nodded at the floor where her little bed had been, and she sat down also.

"No, they didn't beat me. They were just spiteful, mocking, and they paid next to nothing."

"You wish you were back with them now, do you?"

"Yes. I don't mean to be ungrateful, because I am. I don't know where I would have run to if I hadn't tripped over Sally. But I had a bed in Regent's Park; I was warm and fed. I suppose this is my lesson for being dissatisfied with my lot."

"Don't be stupid, why shouldn't you be dissatisfied with your lot? Why shouldn't we all be dissatisfied with our lots? The only people who need to be satisfied with their lot is them as look down on us all. Them who want us to fetch, carry and shovel up their mess for nothing more than a hot meal and a place to sit out of the rain. They're the ones who should be satisfied, but they never are. I wouldn't go torturing yourself with silly ideas that this is your punishment. This is just the way it is, isn't it? People like us, we should *always* be dissatisfied with our lot, believe me."

As advice went, it almost resonated. Perhaps Harry was right; perhaps it was a natural state of being for people who were raised with nothing. Perhaps she wasn't so different from everybody else.

"I suppose you're right," she said after some moments of silence.

"I am right. I'm right about a lot of things, and you could do a lot worse than listen to me, that's for certain. Look, I don't know what they taught you in that place in Regent's Park, but you've got to remember who you are. You've got to remember that survival has to be fought for in this life for the likes of you and me; fine feelings won't get the job done. You've got to be prepared to do whatever it takes to survive, don't you see that?"

"I suppose so," she said cautiously, wondering where this conversation was leading.

"You do want to survive, don't you?"

"You mean... avoid the gallows?"

"No, forget the gallows. There're a hundred and one

other things out there that will kill you first, believe me. My old dad used to say that if the gallows don't get you, poverty will. He was my father and all, but I'm not gonna let either of those two things get me round the throat, if you take my meaning. I might be poor, but I know how to survive. Poverty won't get me, and you shouldn't let it get you either. Like I said, you have to be prepared to do whatever it takes to survive, I know I am."

He was staring at her intently, and she wished she knew exactly what he was getting at. Surely, he didn't mean to have her living in the way that Franklin Wakefield had expected her to! How was it possible for her life to keep getting worse and worse?

"As much as I want to survive, there are things that I won't do. If you think that I'm going to... Just for money, just for..." Her throat tightened, and she began to panic.

"What?" Harry said, looking at her askance. "What do you think I'm talking about, girl?" he said, realisation clearly beginning to dawn.

"The same as Franklin Wakefield expected of me, don't you?"

"I don't know, what was it that Franklin Wakefield expected you to do?" he asked, his tone suggestive of a little teasing.

"What do you think?" she said a little angrily.

"And that's why you killed him, was it? How did you end up in such a situation if you weren't prepared to make your money on your back? Oh, don't look at me like that, Miss hoity-toity, just answer the blooming question." he said and chuckled, the friendly-sounding chuckle of hours before.

"He tricked me into that situation, Harry. As I said, I was dissatisfied with my employment, and he got to hear of it. Anyway, he offered me a job as a housekeeper, working in his house in Camden Town. Only, when he collected me from Regent's Park, he didn't drive me to Camden Town, he drove me here to Southwark. He drove me here to a rotten, stinking tavern and expected me to lay down with the ugly fat landlord."

"The Dog and Duck?" Harry said, surprising her, unsettling her; was she telling him too much? In the end, what did it matter? He already knew enough about her to send her to the gallows; she might just as well say it all out loud and get it off her chest.

"Yes, the Dog and Duck. Wakefield told me I was to be employed as his housekeeper, but as he dragged me into the tavern, he told me that he'd lied. He didn't need me as a housekeeper, and he even laughed at me for thinking I was good enough for such a job. And that was when I realised what it was that he expected me to do. He carried me upstairs and threw me down on a bed, and that's when the landlord came in," she said and shuddered.

"Yes, I can believe that. There's always a prosy or two at the Dog and Duck, and the landlord always gets the first taste."

"He was such an ugly, disgusting man," she said with vehemence, picturing it clearly and remembering her revulsion as if she was right back there in that moment. "He was so drunk that when I pushed him away, he fell. That's when I ran for the stairs, but Franklin Wakefield wouldn't let me past... I shoved him so that I could escape."

"And he fell down the stairs, did he? Likely broke his

neck, I suppose," Harry said a little too gleefully for her liking.

"Yes, he fell down the stairs. So, you see, I won't do just about anything to survive. At least I won't do that," she said, holding his gaze and glaring at him, hoping to impress upon him that she would fight to the death if she had to. She didn't have much in this life, but she certainly wasn't going to let go of the right over her own body.

"Now, you just wait a minute, girl!" Harry said and looked suddenly affronted. "You surely didn't think that I was going to expect something like that, did you? I might be a crook; in fact, I'll hold my hands up to that, but you're just a kid. I know there's some as think that a girl your age is old enough, but not me. In a year or two, maybe, but that ain't my game. Rats are my game, Jane. Rats are my survival. So, you'll be able to sleep with your eyes closed instead of your eyes open now, won't you? Now, you know the truth and everything," he said and seemed to relax again, laughing, finding a curious humour in it all.

"I'm sorry, I didn't mean to offend you, Harry, but after the day I've had, that's the one thing I'm absolutely determined about; the one thing I know I'd rather die before I gave into."

"Spirited little thing, aren't you? I reckon it's a shame that you're just too big to fit through the windows. Mind you, I'll still put you to good use, don't you worry."

"What good use?" she asked, wanting to know exactly what was expected of her before she settled down again for the rest of the night.

"You can help me get the best out of Sally, that's what. She ain't got no partner at the moment, that's why I leave her overseeing it all. But now you can be her lookout, can't you? I can get the best out of the child before she gets much bigger."

"I see," Jane said, feeling relieved and guilty all at once.

Relieved that Harry Newland, as rough and immoral as he was, wasn't the same sort of man that Franklin Wakefield was, and guilty that she would be perpetuating the misery of these children by helping him in his wicked, dishonest games.

"Whatever it is, you just swallow it down, Jane. I've

had enough of your bleeding-heart tonight, and that's the truth. Don't you go making me sorry that I offered to let you live here."

He began to laugh, then let out a mock sigh of exasperation that almost made her feel relaxed. But not so relaxed that she would ever think that she was there on account of a kindly offer. He told her that she lived there, but she understood, almost immediately, that her silence depended upon that.

And so, whether she liked it or not, Jane was going to have to work hard. The only difference this time would be that her hard work wouldn't result in a bed and her own little room, but a blanket on the floor of a cold and damp basement with the occasional crust of bread thrown her way by the rat catcher with the dirty hands.

CHAPTER EIGHT

It was the first time in the six months that Jane had stayed with Harry Newland that one of the children had come close to being caught. Even though Jane acted as Sally's lookout, she always made sure she knew where the other six children were. How Harry's devious little operation hadn't been rumbled by now was beyond her, for the children certainly did make a suspicious sight as they wandered along carrying the wriggling bags in the darkness.

However, it all seemed to work. Jane had to admit a grudging admiration for Sally and the rest of them, they were fearless as they worked. They climbed in through windows, let themselves in through basement doors which had been carelessly left unlocked, and even shinned up drainpipes looking for a way into every building they trespassed within.

Sally, despite being not yet seven years old, was as skilful and silent as a cat when she went about her business. Jane had seen her sliding through impossibly narrow gaps, climb up walls and pipes when there seemed hardly a foothold to be had, and she had even managed to go in through an upstairs window of a fine terraced house without being seen.

Theirs was the night now, the daytime and sunshine were for people who lived differently; better. Yes, Jane did go out in the daytime now and again, but her nocturnal activities meant that she slept through the best of the day, that glorious cool freshness of an early morning. She began to feel like an animal of some kind; an owl, a fox, some creature whose survival could only be sought in the hours of darkness.

On that particular night, there'd been something of a bright moon. Jane had begged Harry to let the children have a night off, it was too bright, she insisted, and he didn't want to risk them being caught, did he? She'd even gone as far as to frame it in the sort of terms a man like Harry would understand. If he lost the children, he would have to train up new ones and what would he do for money in the meantime? He would have to go to so much effort and perhaps even a little expense to get himself back to where he was. But Jane hadn't bargained for his rampant greed, his determination to have the rats set in the hopes that he would be called upon soon enough to remove them. And so, the children had wandered off into the moonlit streets, carrying their little bags of wriggling devils.

Jane always kept to the shadows, always finding a nearby alleyway from which to peer out and watch Sally make her way into the building of choice that night. On this particular night, however, Sally hadn't been able to find her way in. The window which Harry had assured them was always open just a little was firmly closed against the coolness of the night. However, Sally knew better than to give up; she knew better than to go back with the rats still struggling in the bag. And so, spying a sash window a little ajar on the floor above, Sally had decided to try her luck there.

She was climbing up a rusted iron drainpipe, a poorly fitted drainpipe whose brackets looked as if they might give way at any moment. The whole thing gave Jane a dreadful sense of foreboding as she watched the small, skinny girl shin her way up as she clung tightly to the sack of rats.

"What is she going to do when she gets there? Surely, that is somebody's bedroom!" Jane said under her breath, wishing that she could somehow make her feelings known to Sally. When Sally had climbed level with the partially open sash window, she paused and leaned sideways. Jane held her breath, fearing that something would happen and the child would fall to her death. However, she couldn't tear her eyes away and simply watched helplessly as Sally peered in through the window.

Jane could just tell from her mannerisms that there were people inside sleeping. Of course, there were, why else would the window be a little open if not for the comfort of somebody asleep inside? Undeterred however, Sally untied the string at the top of the bag with her teeth, still holding onto it and the drainpipe at the same time. Then, unbelievably, she used one hand to hold on to both the drainpipe and the top of the sack, reaching in and pulling out the first of the rats. She held it by the tail, just as Harry always did, and then carefully slid her hand through the open window and silently set the creature free. Showing no signs of fear or nerves, Sally repeated the process until all four rats had been released into the domain of the unsuspecting householders.

As soon as Sally began to climb down, Jane let out a sigh of relief. The child had just about reached the bottom when the first shout came, almost surprising Jane clean out of the wits. She looked up, fully expecting to see an angry man at the bedroom window where the rats had just been released, but there was nobody there. Then she heard running feet and loudly blown whistles and realised that the peelers must be out. They must have seen her little charge from afar shinning down the drainpipe and had called out before giving chase. Sally didn't wait for any direction from Jane, she simply took to her heels and disappeared into the moonlit night. Jane walked back down the alley, trying to keep out of sight as two policemen tore past, not noticing her as they chased the little girl into the night.

Still keeping to the shadows, Jane looked up in time to see a man, a very fine-looking man, staring out of the bedroom window that Sally had just been peering in through. He was looking curiously out into the street, his eyes following the progress of the peelers as they disappeared out of sight. He seemed curious and nothing more, clearly having no idea that the very beginning of a rat infestation had been let loose in his home that night. No doubt when the vile creatures had been given time to breed a little, the poor man would be only too aware of it.

Finally, the man disappeared back inside his bedroom, closing his sash window against the cool night air. There was nothing left for Jane to do but slowly make her way back to the basement, hoping against all hope that she would find Sally there safe and sound.

Darting swiftly up and down back alleys that she now knew better than the back of her hand, Jane satisfied herself that the rest of the children had performed their nightly duty without detection of any kind. She watched as they each made their stealthy progress home, being sure to keep her wits about her so that she would be the first to know if she herself was being watched.

Acting as a silent shepherd, Jane wondered what sort of person she had become. She was stealthy, even a little devious, pitting her wits against the peelers night after night and always winning. This wasn't her; these were not her values. For all that Harry Newland had given her a certain amount of security, there would always be a part of her which hated him fervently. She would hate him for what he had made her, she would hate him for holding her darkest secret against her and manipulating her in a way which made her feel helpless, powerless. But where would this get her? This was just one night in so many that had passed and so many more that were yet to come. If she thought the same thoughts every night, she'd never know a minute's peace.

She watched as the little ones made their way one by one into the basement and stayed where she was for a while so that she could be sure that the basement wasn't being watched. After ten minutes, she made her own way inside.

"So?" Harry said the moment she made her way right inside.

"I watched them all home, nobody was following. I've been outside for ten minutes or more, and it's as silent as the grave out there," Jane said, marvelling at the way she knew exactly what it was he wanted to hear. She spoke in his terms now, giving every appearance of caring about the things he cared about.

"You were lucky this time, Sally," he said in an angry tone. At the mention of Sally's name, Jane sighed loudly with relief, and Harry looked at her askance.

"She made it," Jane said, one hand on her chest as she gave a brief and silent prayer of thanks for the child's safe return. "She did well, Harry," Jane went on, keen to spare the child any more upset that night. "The window was closed, the downstairs window that you said would be open. Anyway, she didn't give up. This child shinned up the drainpipe and released the rats one by one through a partially open bedroom window."

"For God's sake, now they'll know what our game is!" he said, angry still. Jane knew she had to find some other way to appease him.

"No, they've no idea at all. After Sally set off to lead the peelers a merry dance, I stayed where I was. I kept a watch on the house, kept my ears open, I did," she said, slipping easily into the parlance of the street. "The only thing that woke the man of the house was the peelers yelling and running past. He looked out of his sash window, nosy and nothing more, and then calmly pulled the window closed and went back to his bed. The rats must've made their way into hiding immediately. Whether they did or whether they didn't, the man certainly didn't see Sally. She's as quiet as a mouse and as quick as a cat, and that's the truth," Jane said, appalled by her own words but knowing that they were necessary to give the child a little peace and safety that night.

"Well, you did yourself proud then, Sal!" he said, his mood changing so fast that Jane could hardly believe what she was seeing.

"I set them off quiet, Harry. And I kept my eye on the man the whole time. He was fast asleep as I let go of those rats, I swear he was. And his big fat wife was snoring like a horse. If a man can sleep through that, he can sleep through anything, can't he?" Sally said and laughed, seeming almost confident.

However, as Harry turned his attention from Sally, Jane could see that the poor child was anything but confident. She had not only narrowly escaped the peelers, but she'd narrowly escaped Harry's wrath. Despite her cockney chatter, her flat pigeon chest proudly thrust forward, little Sally had been absolutely terrified. It made Jane sick to see it, and every instinct urged her to wrap her arms around the child and soothe her, keep her safe. But those were finer feelings, and a bleeding heart and Harry wouldn't put up with any of that nonsense.

An hour later, and all the children were sound asleep. Jane watched them from her own pile of blankets on the cold floor, awestruck that such an eventful night hadn't kept them all awake, most particularly Sally. However, Sally was snoring, just as the man's fat wife had earlier. Jane smiled, certain that Sally's childish, gentle snores likely did not compare to the ones the child had described in her retelling of the night's events.

"You ought to be getting to sleep, didn't you?" Harry said, surprising her that he too was still awake.

"I'm just a bit rattled, Harry, that's all," she said, wondering how it was she managed to have something of a relationship with a man she so despised. There were times when they all seemed like a curious sort of family, with Harry as the father and Jane as the mother. It felt normal now, almost a little comforting at times, and Jane hated herself for it. Harry Newland was a devious man who kept half-starved children so that he might use them for his own gain. And yet, her own need for warmth, for human interaction, was so great that it appeared, at times, that Harry would do; Harry Newland would just about fit the bill.

"You did all right though, I'll give you that. It's the first near-miss since you've been with us, isn't it? Yeah, you did all right. I reckon you've come on in leaps and bounds since you first came here to me. I reckon I might have another job in mind for you now. Your talents are wasting out their night after night acting as Sally's lookout."

"What job?" Jane asked, immediately sitting up and reaching for her shawl, pulling it tightly around her.

"Oh, not that again!" Harry said and snorted with laughter. "Don't get your knickers in a twist, girl, I've already told you that *that* ain't my game. No, I've got another plan for you altogether."

"What plan?" Jane asked, determined to hear it before she could allow herself to settle down again.

"Well, it involves you smartening up and going to one of those nice posh houses you're so fond of working in." He laughed, hardly seeming to care about the noise he was making whilst the children who had risked everything for him slept.

"Posh houses? Harry, what are you talking about?"

"Put it this way, girl, for a little while at least, I think you'll be going back into service again." Harry grinned at her before pulling his blankets up tight around his ears and closing his eyes. "Good night, Jane," he said, putting an end to the conversation in a way Jane knew she couldn't argue with.

As she settled back down herself, she knew she wouldn't sleep. Jane would be awake all night wondering what fresh horror the new day would bring.

CHAPTER NINE

"Fiona Radcliffe?" Jane said the following day as she looked down at the austere, but neat dark grey dress Harry had made her put on. "But who is she?"

"She's a widow, Jane, a very wealthy one at that. Her husband died a year or two back and left her an enormous inheritance. A woman in charge of her own house like that doesn't want rats running around now, does she?" Harry said with a greedy smile which sickened Jane to the very core of her being; why were these men all so predatory?

"Then why not just do what you normally do? Why not just have one of the children set the rats loose in her house?" Jane asked, knowing that she wasn't going to like the answer.

"Because Fiona Radcliffe seems to be determined to keep such things out. There's never an open window, never a door left carelessly unlocked. The basement hatches are padlocked tight. It seems she lives in some fear of invasion from the outside like most women do when they're suddenly all alone."

Jane could certainly sympathise with that; she knew what it was to be all alone and afraid. More than ever, she didn't want a part in any of this. If this Fiona Radcliffe, whoever she was, wanted to keep rats and predators at bay, who was Jane to spoil that for her?

"Then wouldn't it just be easier to go to somebody who isn't quite so careful, Harry? I mean, you had to buy this dress, didn't you? You've gone to some expense, I don't understand why." Suddenly, it was important to her to try to protect this woman, to protect her from one of so many predatory men in London. "Why go to the bother when there are so many easier properties to infest?"

"Because this woman has an almost endless supply

of money and an even greater amount of fear. I reckon a woman like that would pay through the nose, don't you? And it's not just going to be a handful of rats this time and a vague hope that they'll breed a bit, I can tell you. It's going to be a sudden invasion of almost half my stock! What do you say to that? Clever, eh?" Harry said and looked truly pleased with himself.

The whole business of planting rats in people's homes was appalling to Jane and had been from the very beginning. There was, however, something about this particular plan which seemed so very much worse. She knew that Harry was a low character; she'd never thought him anything else. But this seemed to drag him lower somehow, the idea that he had cleverly planned out every part of it, that he had gone to some lengths to find a woman who was, by his own admission, recently bereaved and greatly afraid. This wasn't just survival, this was cruelty. How could Jane be a part of this plan when she already felt so much sympathy with this woman?

"I still don't see how you're going to get so many rats into the building if everything is so carefully locked at night," she said, knowing that she was bordering on insubordination and may feel his wrath.

"Because I'll have a woman on the inside, won't I? You'll be there, a permanent fixture, or so they'll think. You will be there to meet me... to take the rats into the house yourself. Now, I don't know if it'll be the middle of the night or the middle of the day, I need a little time to work out the details. You'll probably be there for a good long while before I set the plan into action. For one thing, they need to trust you. For another, I need to watch the house for a while and decide on the best way to go about it. All you need to do for now is make sure you get the bleedin' job and work hard enough that they don't have any thoughts of dismissing you. Because, believe me, if you get dismissed from there, or if you fail to get the job in the first place, you'll be letting me down."

"Letting you down? But what if they don't need any more servants? What if they don't take young women in from the street with no references? How is that my fault?"

"You'll go to the house and around to the servants' entrance," Harry said, as if both bored and exasperated with her. "You'll look clean and respectable in your new dress, your hair will be tidy, and you'll be speaking in that nice little voice of yours. You'll tell them that you don't have any references because you've not long come from the orphanage. You've worked hard in the orphanage, and you know how to keep the kitchen nice and tidy, how to help prepare food, how to shovel horse manure if that's what's required of you. It's down to you to be persuasive, Jane. It's down to you to put the effort in."

"I think I've already put in enough effort for you," Jane said, her anger and disgust making her a little careless.

Harry seized the back of her neck, his large hand squeezing her hard and painfully.

Jane tipped her head back further and further, knowing that to pull away would be all the more painful. But whatever she did, he just squeezed harder and harder, that ugly chuckle of his so menacing, so self-satisfied with the upper hand he held.

"Just you remember, Jane Ashford, that not only do I know your name and what you did, but I have the name of the man you killed. I'm out and about and a man who knows things, girl. I know that the peelers are still looking for the young woman who murdered Franklin Wakefield, leaving him broken-necked at the bottom of the stairs in the Dog and Duck. The only thing they don't know is her name, isn't it? But I know the name of the girl, don't I? And whilst the peelers might not like me much, they'll bloomin' well listen to me, won't they? When I turn up there and give them the name of the little orphan girl who murdered such a fine gentleman, they'll be looking for you. They won't need to look far, though, because I'll drag you to them. I'll walk you right up the steps of the gallows if it comes to it. Now then, are you listening to me, girl?" he said, his voice a sneer.

Even though he was behind her, Jane could picture his face. His mouth always narrowed to almost nothing when he spoke in that foul, threatening tone of voice. She'd seen it more than enough; she'd seen him subject the children to it as well as herself. And as for his threat, well, who wouldn't believe him? He knew so much about her now that he owned her. He owned her and he always would, she could see that now.

"Yes," she said, tears of pain streaming down her face.

He let go of her immediately, pushing her hard in the back away from him. She stumbled forward but kept her balance, turning fast and instinctively in case he was advancing upon her for another attack. However, Harry was simply standing there looking at her, his head tilted on one side as he waited for her to speak.

"I'll do it, I'll try my hardest to get employment in Fiona Radcliffe's house," Jane said, despising him so much that she wished he was dead. However, she was quickly reminded of how things had ended the last time she'd wished a man dead. Her wish had come true, and her life had become even worse.

"That's the spirit," Harry said, mocking her. "So, you get yourself a job inside that house, and you work hard. And don't you go thinking of getting comfortable there, of turning your back on me, because you know what I'll do, don't you?"

"Yes."

"I'll be watching, and I'll find the right time to speak to you. I'll make contact with you to let you know I'm out there and watching. When the time is right, I'll give you your instructions for getting the rats and taking them into the house. Up until that time, all you need to concentrate on is becoming a trusted servant, do you see? All you have to do is work as a maid. You've done that before, and you can do it again, can't you?"

"Yes, I can," Jane said, wondering if her entire life was going to be this awful.

What would happen to her if she was discovered taking a sack full of rats into her new employer's home, assuming she managed to get work in that house in the first place? She would end up in the deepest trouble and probably in jail. When that happened, perhaps all would be discovered about the part she'd played in Franklin Wakefield's untimely death. One way or another, it seemed ever more likely that Jane's life really would end at the gallows. If only the short slice of life between now and that awful eventuality could at least have some joy in it. Just one day, just an hour, even just a few minutes. If only she could have that much happiness in life at least.

But, of course, her experience of life so far told her clearly that this was probably the biggest and most unrealistic dream of them all.

CHAPTER TEN

Fiona Radcliffe's house was in Covent Garden, the other side of the river and a good forty minutes' walk from the basement in Southwark. The idea of being so far away from Harry might have given her some measure of peace for a while had it not been for the idea that, at any given moment, he might well be watching the house, watching her. It was as if she had been handed a little piece of freedom with one hand only to have the other hand take it back again.

The house in Covent Garden was very fine indeed. It was a large house made of white stone in the Georgian style, with a wide black painted front door and immense stone pillars holding up a canopy above. It was on three floors, with added basement and attics. It was a tall building, its roof clearly marked against the pale blue sky.

Like all such houses in London, Jane knew that it would be so much bigger inside than it looked on the outside. She realised there would be a good many servants employed within. Even from the outside, the house looked twice as large as that of her previous employers in Regent's Park. With any luck, they would be in need of more servants than they already had.

Although she was making her own way to the house, Jane knew that Harry was watching. She turned once or twice to see where he was, but he was nowhere to be seen. But seen or not, she knew he was there observing her, she could feel it.

A part of her wanted to walk right past that house, to take to her heels and run. However, Harry was fit, strong, and wily. He'd find her wherever she went and, if he didn't, the peelers would once they finally had the name of the girl who had murdered Franklin Wakefield.

With a heavy heart and a sense of an inevitability

that couldn't be fought, Jane made her way to the back of the house in search of the servants' entrance. When she reached it, she knocked on the door before looking down at her dress. She set her bag down with a few things that Harry had bought for her, a nightgown and stockings and such the like, and straightened the neat grey dress. Then she raised her hand to her soft brown hair, neatly tied back in a bun. Just as she bent down and picked up her bag again, the door opened and a smart, vexed looking man of advancing years squinted out at her.

"What do you want?" he said, his accent just like her own; most definitely London but with an attempt to soften the harshness.

"Sir, I am looking for work. I'm a very hard worker, and I am prepared to take on any duty required in the house," she said, trying to refine her own accent further still.

"My mistress is not in the habit of taking in just anybody off the street, girl. Now then, take yourself away elsewhere. My advice to you would be to present yourself at a much smaller establishment, somewhere where they are a little less fussy about who they employ," he said in a cold tone of voice.

"Sir, I will take the lowest job on the staff, anything, I only want a chance," Jane spoke quickly, determined not to have him close the door in her face as she remembered only too well the painful grip on the back of her neck and Harry Newland's promise to turn her in if she didn't get herself employment there.

"Oh, come on, Mr Morton, can't you see the girl is trying? And she already sounds much cleverer than half the maids here," the voice sounded amused and came from a rather handsome young man who gently pushed his way past Mr Morton and out of the house.

He had dark hair and bright green eyes and was dressed like a gentleman, making her utterly confused as to his appearance there at the servants' entrance.

"I would have let you out the front door, sir," Mr Morton said, hardly bothering to hide his disapproval.

"Not to worry, Morton," the young man said and laughed brightly. "I only came down to see if the cook would let me have a couple of her wonderful scones before I disappear home again. I couldn't be bothered to walk back up the stairs, if I'm honest. Not to worry, my dear man, as I said. It's not like I'm going to tell tales on you, is it?"

"Very good, Mr Sinclair," Mr Morton said, with not even half an ounce of amusement inside him. It was clear that the man, most likely the butler she thought, was waiting for the curious Mr Sinclair to take his leave before he finally dismissed her. With that in mind, Jane looked briefly at the young man in a somewhat pleading way.

"It is a bit tight of you, Mr Morton, to try to send the girl away when she is trying so hard. Do you not applaud her for taking a chance and coming to such a fine house? But I can see you do not, for you have already poured scorn upon her for that. But we all have to start somewhere, do we not? Why not aim high, that's what I say? Why not do the best for yourself that you can? I'm sure there have been times when you have done what is the very best for yourself, Mr Morton, haven't you?" He turned to look squarely at the butler, seeming to stand at her side whilst he did so.

"I have to look out for the best interests of my

mistress, Mr Sinclair," Mr Morton said as if desperately searching for a reasonable excuse to send Jane away, despite this young man's attempt at interference.

"Well, I'm sure my dear Fiona would at least like the opportunity to have a look at the girl, don't you? She seems such a bright young thing," Mr Sinclair went on, and it was clear that he was enjoying himself now, pleased to have an opportunity to tease the stuffy butler.

"Mrs Prescott has said nothing about needing any more maids, Mr Sinclair," Mr Morton went on, seeming now desperate for a reason to have Jane sent on her way.

Jane couldn't help but think that this was now a battle of wills between Mr Morton and Mr Sinclair. She had just been a minor irritation to the butler only minutes before, but now she thought she was all but forgotten in the austere old man's determination to win this particular argument. For her part, Jane was firmly on Mr Sinclair's side. Much apart from seeming to be on her side himself, there was something nice about Mr Sinclair. He was a few years older than Jane, perhaps seventeen or eighteen, and he carried a little bundle of books under one arm, tied with a strap to keep them together. Having learnt to read herself when she was at the orphanage, Jane had always longed to own a book or two herself.

"I'm sure that the housekeeper is always in want of extra hands, Mr Morton. Perhaps I ought to call her, have her come out and look at this girl and see if it's in her interests to approach Mrs Radcliffe with a request to give her a trial at least," Mr Sinclair said, clearly still amused but not quite as amused as he had been. Jane was very much under the impression now that he was determined to have his way as much as Mr Morton was determined that he not.

Jane wondered at the relationship between this young man and the lady of the house. He had, after all, first described her as *my dear Fiona*. Whilst he was being a little more cautious in his address now by calling her *Mrs Radcliffe*, surely his opinion would have some sway in that house. Perhaps he was even a relative, although Harry certainly hadn't mentioned that Fiona Radcliffe had any children.

With a sigh of annoyance, Mr Morton turned and made his way back into the house, leaving the door open. Jane stood there, wondering what it all meant and feeling both afraid and embarrassed at once.

“Come along, my dear, let’s not stand out here,” Mr Sinclair said, gently taking her arm and guiding her into the basement of the house, the servants’ area. “I am Edgar Sinclair, by the way. Now then, what’s your name?” he said, smiling at her.

“I am Jane, Jane Smith,” she said, using the name that Harry Newland had demanded she use. In what seemed like a rare moment of care, he’d told her that, for her own sake, she would be better off not introducing herself by her real name. Perhaps the peelers had worked it out after all and were already looking for Miss Jane Ashford.

“Well, it’s very nice to meet you, Jane Smith,” Edgar said and smiled at her. “You must forgive dear old Morton, he has dreadful bunions, and they make him a little disagreeable,” he said and winked at her, making her laugh just a little.

“All right, all right, what’s all this?” Mrs Prescott, a woman whose fearful scowl made her look a hundred times colder and more unapproachable than Mrs Coleman had been, strode towards them.

They were standing in a cold, stone-floored lobby area, just outside the kitchen.

"Ah, there you are, my dear Mrs Prescott," Edgar said with such gaiety that Jane knew he was teasing the woman. "This very fine young woman is looking for work, and I thought she might do you very well, my dear. I can already see that she is a bright sort of a girl, just the very thing to help you out, my dear," he went on, smiling.

"As you know, it's not my place to hire and fire, sir. It would have to be the mistress who had the final say," the woman said as if she too was trying to put off Edgar Sinclair's wants. The way her eyes darted to the butler, Jane was certain that her reticence was more to please him than anything. Perhaps she liked him, or perhaps she feared him; either way, Jane was beginning to think she would most certainly be an unwelcome addition to the household as far as these two were concerned. Nonetheless, she had a job to do, and it wouldn't serve her well to let such things worry her.

"Then perhaps you would be so good, my dear Mrs Prescott, as to seek out Mrs Radcliffe and ask her. I'll wait here, my dear," he added, bullying the woman in the most polite and friendly way possible.

"Very well," Mrs Prescott said and sighed before taking her leave. When Mr Morton followed along behind her, Jane had to admit to relief.

"Don't you worry about the two of them, Jane, they are the same with everybody. Obviously, they have a little better status in this house than the rest of the servants, being the butler and the housekeeper, and I rather think it goes to their heads somewhat. But Fiona, *Mrs Radcliffe*, is a very fair woman. I know some of these wealthy widows can be a little cruel to the servants, but Mrs Radcliffe isn't one of them. Just be honest with her, speak with her plainly, and I am sure you will be perfectly all right." He smiled at her, his green eyes seeming so genuine.

The problem was, Jane had seen genuine eyes before, hadn't she? She had fallen foul of men who would be saviours already in her life, hadn't she? Franklin Wakefield had seemed like a decent, honest man, one with a little humour and a nice face. What an awful thing that she now feared the handsome young man who had already done so much to help her. But Jane knew what men were, or at least she did now, and she was certain that not one of them would help simply for the sake of helping. There was always another motive, she was sure of it.

"Do you live here, sir?" Jane asked, feeling she must know if this young man would be in close proximity. She suddenly didn't want him to be, for she might always suspect him of something and never feel a moment's safety.

"No, I am just a friend of the family. Well, a friend of Fiona, Mrs Radcliffe. She is a friend of my aunt, Cora Blythe, and we are both regular visitors to this house. Mrs Radcliffe lost her husband not quite two years ago, you see, and she has suffered greatly on account of it. My Aunt Cora and I do what we can to comfort and support her. So, you will see me around the place, for I am here often," he said and smiled.

"Thank you for your help, sir," Jane said, wishing she knew whether or not she could trust this open-faced young man.

"Not at all, not at all. I don't underestimate the courage it takes to approach a door, knock it, and ask for work. Well, I hear Mrs Prescott's heavy and resistant footsteps approaching," he said and raised his eyebrows amusingly. "I daresay we are now both to stand to attention," he added under his breath.

"The mistress will see her," Mrs Prescott said with an air of annoyance. Jane was certain that her annoyance was for the interfering young man, rather than Jane, but that Jane would likely be the one to suffer for it in the end. Mrs Prescott and Mr Morton had no power to make Edgar Sinclair pay for his interference, but they most certainly would have power over Jane to make her life a misery if that was what they chose to do.

"Then I shall take my leave, my dear Mrs Prescott. Good luck to you, Jane," he said and inclined his head respectfully before turning to let himself out of the servants' entrance.

"Well, come on then, child, my mistress won't wait all day for you!" Mrs Prescott said with a scowl, and Jane realised that it had already begun.

"This is her, Mrs Radcliffe. This is Jane Smith," Mrs Prescott said when she led Jane into a large, beautiful drawing room.

There were wonderful rugs, with such rich and vibrant colours. There were couches and armchairs, all of them covered in either blue or dark grey brocade, some of them in velvet. There was an immense stone fireplace, twice as wide as the fireplace in the drawing room of the Collins' house in Regent's Park.

Mrs Radcliffe was sitting on the couch closest to the fire, perched neatly on one end of it as she studied Jane closely.

Fiona Radcliffe had a nice face. Her golden hair was fading, greying, and gave away her age far more than her smooth, blemish-free skin. Jane suspected her to be somewhere in her early fifties, although she might easily have passed for a woman ten years younger. She had pale blue eyes and something of a sympathetic expression, an expression that Jane hoped she could trust.

"Hello, Jane," Mrs Radcliffe said in a gentle voice.

"Thank you for seeing me, Mrs Radcliffe, I do appreciate it," Jane said, and was pleased when Fiona Radcliffe smiled at her.

"My goodness, what a lovely gentle voice you have," Mrs Radcliffe continued, seeming surprised. "Tell me, where have you worked before?"

"I have never worked in a large house, Mrs Radcliffe, so I'm afraid I don't have any references. I was raised in an orphanage, you see. But I have worked hard in the orphanage, Mrs Radcliffe, and have learned almost all of the skills required for service. They train us very well, the guardians, because it is the responsibility of the orphans to keep the orphanage clean and tidy and to provide the meals. I really would be so very grateful for the opportunity to work in your beautiful home, Mrs Radcliffe," Jane said, realising that this was the moment of truth and somewhat embarrassed to find herself a little tearful.

She knew her tears weren't entirely for herself, but rather for the idea that she was soon to betray this woman with the kindly face and the fading golden hair. This woman who had lost her husband not two years before and was still deep enough in her grief that she required the constant support of her friend and that friend's nephew. Jane felt lower than Harry Newland at that moment and only hoped that Mrs Fiona Radcliffe couldn't see it.

"And it was very brave of you to come here in search of work, Jane. I must admit that I am inclined to give you the opportunity by way of reward for that bravery. Of course, you will be expected to work hard. Mrs Prescott has been the housekeeper here for many years, and she has very high standards. However, if you do as she says and work as hard as you can, I am sure you will be successful. So, welcome to my home, Jane, I hope this works well for the both of us."

"Thank you, Mrs Radcliffe. Thank you very much," Jane said and smiled, turning to look at Mrs Prescott and determined to get on the right side of that woman too. However, there was a steely look in Mrs Prescott's beady eyes which told Jane very clearly that it would take more than a smile to achieve it.

"I will leave it to you to settle Jane in and instruct her, Mrs Prescott," Mrs Radcliffe said by way of dismissing them both.

"Very well, Mrs Radcliffe," Mrs Prescott said and

looked sharply at Jane, inclining with her head towards the door. "Come along, Jane," she said, and Jane, bobbing a small curtsy at her new mistress, turned back to the housekeeper before following her out of the drawing room.

Well, Harry would be very pleased with her indeed. Whatever way she looked at it, however, Jane knew that she could never, ever be pleased with herself.

CHAPTER ELEVEN

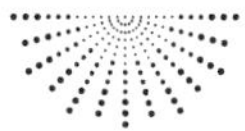

"Right, you can come with me into Covent Garden and carry the bits and pieces I need, Jane," Mrs Prescott said in the cold voice she not only used on Jane but seemed to use on everybody else as well.

Jane had been working at the Radcliffe house for almost two months. In all that time, she had never seen Harry Newland once and almost began to wonder if he had been caught in the act by the peelers and sent to jail. She knew it was wishful thinking, but she was coming to entertain the idea more and more, deriving a certain amount of peace from it.

If such a wonderful thing happened, then surely

Jane would be able to stay in Covent Garden, to live out her life in service and force herself to be a much more contented young woman that she had been in Regent's Park.

The truth was that her new mistress was head and shoulders above her last one. Jane hardly saw her, but when she did, the woman always gave her a smile and had, once or twice, asked her how she was settling in. Still, life was far from easy, for Mrs Prescott seemed to be every bit as spiteful as Mrs Collins had been back in Regent's Park. The only difference between the two women was class and station as far as Jane could tell, for it didn't matter how hard she worked, Mrs Prescott always found some fault with her.

"Yes, Mrs Prescott," Jane said meekly, adopting the tone she instinctively used around the housekeeper.

"Obviously we won't be collecting everything we need for the party, we're only ordering it after all. But there is a little stall at the market where I like to pick up my spices, so you take that basket there," she said, nodding at a large woven basket with a rigid handle in the corner of the kitchen. "And you can carry whatever little bits I intend to bring back with us today. Oh, yes, and you must remind me to pick up a newspaper for Mr Morton.

"Yes, Mrs Prescott," Jane said again.

As much as it was clear that Mrs Prescott didn't like her, she seemed to be giving her jobs of more and more responsibility as each day passed. Jane really had worked hard, throwing herself into things and using hard work as a means of forgetting her awful purpose there and the life which waited for her outside of Mrs Radcliffe's house. With any luck, Mrs Prescott would soon think to send Jane alone on any little errands which she didn't want to do herself. It would give her a little freedom, a few minutes where she was alone at last.

The servants' quarters were nice enough. They were as spartan as servants' quarters anywhere, it was true, but unlike Regent's Park, Jane did not have a room to herself. She shared a room with a girl who, like her, was fourteen. The girl was called Betsy Miller, and while she was pleasant enough, she was a little dull-witted. Since they had been sharing, Jane had begun to feel somewhat responsible for her and often helped her out in her own duties around the house. As nice as it was to have company, Betsy wasn't worth much as an ally. She was already coming to rely on Jane, a responsibility that Jane could well do without. Not only that, but the girl was a romantic creature who talked incessantly about young men, often late into the night. Well, Betsy might well have a romantic heart, but Jane was certain that she never would, and she wasn't at all happy to have to hear the romantic musings night after night.

The only thing of interest that the girl had talked about in the wee small hours had been Edgar Sinclair. Whilst he was, indeed, a regular visitor to the house, a good deal of Jane's first two months had been spent below stairs, and she had seen very little of him. Betsy, however, filled in one or two gaps rather helpfully.

She told Jane that Edgar Sinclair was the nephew of Mrs Cora Blythe, another extraordinarily wealthy widow and a very good friend of Fiona Radcliffe. That was as much information as Betsy parted with regarding Cora Blythe, but of Edgar Sinclair, she spoke at length. How handsome he was, how fine he was, how friendly and funny he was with the servants. And he was kind, too, for he had spent no less than an entire afternoon helping Betsy with her reading. He'd even said that, once she had learned enough about the art, he would let Betsy read one of his books. To a young, dull-witted and ridiculously romantic young woman like Betsy, such a kindly offer was surely the first steppingstone to an outright proposal of marriage. If only Jane could inhabit such a fancy-filled and carefree world herself. If only Jane didn't already know enough about the world to know that it certainly didn't work that way.

However, it had been nice to hear a little something of the young man who'd helped secure her the position she most certainly would not have had the opportunity of if he'd not been there on that day.

The more she heard of him from Betsy, the more Jane was inclined to have a little trust in the young man. That being said, when she hardly ever saw him, she wondered what use that trust was in the end.

"Don't just stand there, girl, get the basket!" Jane was dragged roughly from her reverie by Mrs Prescott's booming voice. "I haven't got all day, Jane. I've things to do, and so have you, so get on with it!"

Jane shook herself and hurried across the kitchen to pick up the basket. It was time to stop thinking about

Edgar Sinclair, or indeed anything else beyond what it was Mrs Prescott wanted of her.

When they reached the market at Covent Garden, Jane realised that, despite having the sour housekeeper for company, she was rather enjoying the little excursion. She hoped it heralded the sign of things to come, for a little while at least; for as long as she was in service to Mrs Radcliffe.

The market was busy, full of life, full of people, full of costermongers shouting left, right, and centre about the goods they were selling. There was something wonderfully vibrant about it and Jane, forgetting the uncertainty of her circumstances for a few moments, allowed herself to be completely immersed. She watched as Mrs Prescott seemed to barter with the impossibly small man who had a wheeled cart full of jars of spices and herbs. Jane kept out of the way; judging from the disagreeable look on Mrs Prescott's face, she was arguing with the man. Jane didn't want anything to spoil those few minutes of enjoyment, most particularly not Mrs Prescott and her angry ways.

"Come with me." The voice was breathed into her ear at the same time as a strong hand gripped her upper arm. Jane was being propelled towards an alleyway just a few yards away, and she had all but reached it by the time she realised that her assailant was none other than Harry Newland.

"Harry, Mrs Prescott will be looking for me. If you want to see me turned out of that house, this is the best way to do it. She watches me like a hawk, she hates me, and she is looking for any excuse to have Mrs Radcliffe get rid of me."

"Don't get your knickers in a twist," Harry said and gave his snarling laugh. "Although, I'm pleased to see that you're being a good little girl and working as hard as you can to try and keep that job of yours," he went on.

"She won't be long before she comes looking for me, Harry," Jane said desperately. She wanted Harry to go away, to cease to be a part of her world. Seeing his face was just the awful confirmation that he wasn't languishing in jail somewhere, much as she had hoped. He had ruined those few moments; he had ruined them before Mrs Prescott had even had a chance to do that herself.

"I just wanted you to know that I'm still here, still

watching. You've done well, working your way into that house and staying there, I'll give you that. I'll keep watching, I'll keep waiting, but you need to find a way to let that old bat over there send you out on your own. Once you start going out on your own, that's when I'll get my chance to hand over the rats."

"In broad daylight? But what am I supposed to do with a sack full of rats in broad daylight?"

"You'll think of something," Harry said and gave a horrible, derisory laugh. "Anyway, best get back to the old bat, hadn't you?"

"Yes," Jane said and started to walk away from him. However, he gripped her arm hard and dragged her backwards again.

"You're hurting me," she said and glared at him.

"Don't you go getting too comfortable in the house, girl. You belong to me, just you remember that. You'll be working there for as long as I say you will and no longer, so don't be getting any big ideas. Don't get any ideas about leaving me, about giving me up, about turning me in, because I will see you swinging from a rope, do you hear me?"

"I hear you. I always hear you," she said and sharply pulled her arm away and hurried out of the alleyway.

By the time she had Mrs Prescott back in sight, it was to see that the woman was still engrossed in the pastime of trying to beat the costermonger down to his lowest price. What did she care, it wasn't her money, was it? Not that any of this mattered; all that mattered was that Mrs Prescott hadn't seen Jane with Harry. If he wanted her to do this job, he ought to leave her alone. Nothing was sure to see her turned out of the house than Mrs Prescott having some tale to tell the mistress.

"Well, that dreadful little man!" Mrs Prescott said, carrying small paper bags which were no doubt filled with assorted herbs and spices. "I told him this was for Mrs Fiona Radcliffe, and do you know what he said to me?" Mrs Prescott said, her furious eyes fixed firmly on Jane's, her raised eyebrows suggesting that she expected a response.

"No, what did he say, Mrs Prescott?" Jane asked in a tone she hoped was soothing enough to bring Mrs Prescott back down to earth.

"He said *I don't care if it's for Queen Victoria herself!*

She pays, and your Mrs pays too! Well, what an ungrateful little beast!"

"Yes, Mrs Prescott." Jane wondered if she would spend the rest of her time in Covent Garden saying *yes, Mrs Prescott.*

"To bring the Queen into it! Really, men like him are just one inch away from the gutter!"

"Yes, Mrs Prescott."

"Right, well, we'd better get to the butcher and have a word with him about all the meat we need for the party. I hope he will be ready to deliver it tomorrow because I'm in no mood to put up with any of his nonsense either," Mrs Prescott said and marched away leaving Jane to follow along in her wake.

The party, in the end, was quite a low-key affair. There were several guests, it was true, but none of them was due to spend the night, and none of them seemed to be of the type to make a fuss about anything. It was quiet, rather than poorly attended, and a very far cry from the sort of parties that Jane had had to help with in Regent's Park for Mildred and Rupert Collins. There was none of that awful upper-class braying laughter, no obvious displays of arrogance. All in all, Jane was glad for the opportunity to work above stairs for a while.

The guests were in the dining room, where a lavish meal was to be served. Of course, Jane wasn't going to be serving, and she was rather glad of it. The very thought of it made her nervous and shaky. Instead, she was going to spend a good part of the evening going up and down the stairs, carrying food up, carrying empty platters back. It would be tiring, but it would certainly be a break from the scullery and the kitchen.

Jane had been given a black dress to wear for the evening, the same as the housemaids wore. Over the top of it, she wore a pristine white apron and a small black and white hat to go with it. Well, it wasn't a hat, exactly, but rather a smart little band that was pinned to her hair. It might well be a maid's uniform, but it was the nicest, highest quality outfit she'd ever worn in her life and Jane felt wonderful wearing it.

Below stairs, she had simply continued to wear the

dark grey dress that Harry had bought her with a rough grey cotton canvas apron over the top. Given that she was mostly helping to prepare food for the cook, up to her elbows in hot soapy water washing sheets, or sweeping through the entire servants' area, nothing smarter than that was required.

For the first two dishes that she had brought up the stairs, Jane had been too nervous to look about the dining room too much. However, when she brought in a covered serving dish of hot potatoes, she realised she was beginning to relax. She set them down on the serving sideboard, just as she had been instructed to do earlier by Mrs Prescott.

Mrs Prescott herself was still below stairs, barking instructions and losing her temper all over the place. Upstairs, proceedings were being conducted by none other than Mr Morton. His dark trousers and tailcoat seemed blacker than ever, more pristine, and his glare ever more steely. He remained straight-backed and a little proud as he stood at the side of the serving table, silently watching as the young footman began to serve up the food.

With Mr Morton's attention suitably drawn away from her, Jane gave herself a moment or two to study the room. Mrs Radcliffe sat at the head of the table, smiling serenely and talking in gentle tones with her guests. At her side sat a woman a little older, perhaps fifty-five, her own dark hair liberally sprinkled with great strands of white. She was neat and tidy, but there was something about her which suggested that she was of the approachable variety of upper-class woman, rather like Mrs Radcliffe herself. As Mrs Radcliffe turned now and again to talk to her, to smile at her warmly, Jane realised that this must surely be Mrs Cora Blythe, the woman Betsy had claimed was Mrs Radcliffe's dearest friend.

Just as Jane had decided upon the woman's identity, she realised that she was being stared at. Her eyes wandered along the table until they fell upon Edgar Sinclair, seeming strangely alone in the middle of the table. Each of his nearest neighbours was turned in the opposite direction and engaged in conversations with others. He reminded her of a great rock in a pond somehow, standing out, just sitting there. Their eyes met, and Edgar flashed a broad and brief grin. Knowing she could do no other, Jane gave him an even briefer smile of her own, something that nobody else might notice if they happened to look at her.

She hurried from the room, quickly making her way

back downstairs for the next serving bowl or platter that Mrs Prescott had ready for her. It was going to be a long night, and she needed all her concentration. Staring at Edgar Sinclair and wondering about the nature of the man certainly wasn't going to help.

Some hours later, when all the guests had made their way into the drawing room for brandy and other such similar delights, Jane found herself alone clearing the last of the plates. At first, when the dining room had become empty, servants seemed to swarm about the place like a plague of locusts, removing plates and platters, clearing away knives and forks. However, now that there were just a few last odds and ends to be gathered, Mrs Prescott had sent her back alone to finish it.

"I thought I might find you here." Edgar Sinclair peered around the door, his head seeming entirely disembodied as it floated there between the door and the frame.

"Mrs Prescott has sent me up to clear the last of the things, Mr Sinclair," Jane said politely.

"Well, there's no harm in me keeping you company for a minute or two, is there?"

"No, I daresay not," Jane said, all the while fighting an urge to tell him to leave her be. If either Mr Morton or Mrs Prescott found her there alone with one of Mrs Radcliffe's guests, no doubt, they would find some way to use it against her.

"Well, I suppose in the absence of any greater encouragement, I shall just blunder in anyway," Edgar said and laughed as he made his way into the dining room and pushed the door to behind him. Jane's old suspicion still lurked deep inside her, and she was relieved that he did not close the door entirely. He walked into the room, taking a seat at the table, and seeing that her own way to the door was clear, Jane relaxed; he wasn't trying to trap her there.

"I hope you enjoyed the dinner party, sir," she said, feeling embarrassed as she fought for some conversation that would be acceptable. What did servants say to a gentleman, a guest in the home of her mistress? Surely, this was most unusual.

"Very much, even the cook's rock-hard little potatoes

were almost palatable." He was laughing mischievously, his boyish face reminding her that he was perhaps no more than two or three years older than she was.

"I'd better not tell her you said that," Jane said, surprising herself by teasing him. "She would chase any man with a broom who has a word to say against her cooking, even a gentleman like yourself," Jane went on and was pleased when he burst out laughing.

"I like you, Jane Smith. I liked your courage when I first met you, and I think I rather like your sense of humour now. Didn't I tell old Mrs Prescott that you were a clever young woman?"

"Yes, you did, and I know I have you to thank for my position here in the house."

"No, you have yourself to thank. It was your courage which brought you here, it is your hard work which has kept you here. I don't doubt that Mrs Prescott gives you a hard time and has probably decided from the word go that she didn't like you, but I see you're already working above stairs."

"Only tonight, sir. Ordinarily, I'm below stairs

working." Jane had gathered the last of the plates and stacked them into a neat pile, ready to take them downstairs. She took the damp cloth from the pocket of her pristine apron and dabbed at a small gravy stain on the tablecloth, anything to keep her occupied whilst Edgar Sinclair was in the room.

He really did look nice. He was wearing black trousers and shoes with a black smart jacket and waistcoat. His shirt was a brilliant white with its stiff collars standing to attention around his neck, held in place by the tie made from a very dark black and rather shiny silk material. He would have looked so dark with his hair being almost black too had it not been for those very fine and very bright green eyes. Perhaps the darkness of his clothes made them stand out all the more, but Jane realised that they were the most handsome, attractive eyes she'd ever seen.

If life hadn't treated her so cruelly and if her opinion of men was not so jaded by the predatory ones she had thus far encountered, Jane might have allowed her deeply buried romantic heart to have its way and imagine herself married to such a beautiful young man. But life *had* treated her cruelly, and she would fight against any idea of romance that her heart might suggest. Instead, she would choose to treat him like an ally for now, for as long as she worked in this house. Beyond that, Jane would not think of him at all.

"Yes, perhaps, but poor old Betsy isn't here tonight carrying food, is she? Even though she works above stairs for a lot of the time, dusting and what have you, Mrs Prescott doesn't trust her on a night like tonight, does she?"

"Mr Sinclair, I like Betsy very much," Jane said, her thinly veiled warning surprising her.

"I like Betsy too, Jane, so you needn't worry that I'm being cruel about her. She works hard, and she is so gloriously butter-fingered that she makes me smile. No, we are rather friends, Betsy and I," he went on, seeming keen for her to know that he was a better man than most in his position. "Being Miss Butterfingers, Betsy would have turned into a bundle of nerves and found a way to tip potatoes all over the place. So, my point is that you should take heart, Miss Jane Smith. You might think that Mrs Prescott doesn't like you very much, and perhaps she doesn't, but she trusts you, and she realises your worth. Perhaps that would keep you here for now at least?"

Keep her here? Why would he care if she stayed or went?

"I suppose I shall be here for as long as Mrs Prescott and Mr Morton can bear the sight of me." She smiled at him, a broad smile that was by way of an apology for her assumptions. "And it's very kind of you to be bothered about it all, sir. I really am very grateful," she went on, so very politely.

"Perhaps you'll be something of a friend of mine, Jane? Like dear old Betsy?" He looked at her, hopefully.

"Yes, that would be nice," Jane said, not really knowing what else to say and blushing suddenly. "Although I can already read, Mr Sinclair."

"I'm not at all surprised that you can read, Jane. Perhaps I will bring you down a book one day next week if you care to read one?"

"Yes, please," Jane said, instantly forgetting every suspicion she might ever have held about the young man. She'd never had a book to read from cover to cover before, only passages from the Bible and various newspapers at the orphanage.

"Well, I suppose I didn't ought to keep you very much longer, or Mrs Prescott will be coming upstairs to look for you," he said and rose to his feet. He surprised her by bowing as if she were some fine young lady rather than one of the household maids. "Take care of yourself, Miss Jane Smith," he added.

"Thank you, sir," she said and curtsied neatly.

"I will see you soon," he smiled and walked to the door, turning back just before he left. "One day next week." And with that, he was gone.

"Right, you go up with Mr Morton and the footman," Mrs Prescott said when Jane had hoped she was about to be released for the night. "The ladies will need help with their coats, and the other maids are busy," she went on, and Jane wondered if Edgar Sinclair had been right; perhaps she was a little more efficient than the rest.

"Yes, Mrs Prescott," Jane said dutifully and followed Mr Morton back up the servants' staircase.

The guests were taking their time to leave, each of them wanting a few minutes with their hostess before they donned their hats, coats, and cloaks, and said good night. Jane had carefully helped two departing ladies into very fine cloaks already and was waiting patiently for Mrs Cora Blythe to be helped into her own. However, Mrs Blythe was still chattering happily with her friend and hostess, and so Jane stood patiently holding her thick, beautiful cloak. She tried to keep her attention to herself as Mr Morton helped Edgar Sinclair into his coat and handed him his top hat. She knew Edgar was looking at her, but she didn't dare risk returning his glance for fear that Mr Morton would have something to say about it.

"Well, a wonderful evening, my dear Fiona," Cora Blythe said and kissed her friend's cheek, a clear sign that she was now ready to leave.

She walked towards Jane, ready to have the housemaid help her on with her cloak. However, when she was but a few steps away, Cora Blythe stopped and stared openly at Jane. She tilted her head a little, narrowing her eyes with curiosity. Jane felt suddenly afraid; no member of the upper classes, apart from Edgar Sinclair, had ever paid her so much attention.

"My dear child, do I know you?" Mrs Blythe asked and then smiled. "You do look so awfully familiar," she went on.

"No, Ma'am, I don't think so," Jane said and blushed.

"Goodness me, where do you think you know Miss Jane Smith from, Aunt Cora?" Edgar said, smiling and clearly enjoying himself.

"Jane Smith? Your name is Jane Smith?" Cora Blythe said and closed her eyes for a moment. "No, I don't think I know any Jane Smith. I must be mistaken, my dear. But really, you do rather strike a chord, really you do." Cora Blythe smiled at her, her eyes as dark brown as it was possible for eyes to be without being black. "Thank you kindly," she went on as Jane helped her into her cloak.

"Well, Aunt Cora, dear Fiona has other guests to say good night to. Come now, take my arm," Edgar said, smiling warmly at his aunt as he held out his arm.

"You're a good boy, Edgar. Such a good boy," Cora said as she took his arm. "Good night, Fiona."

"Good night, Cora, my sweet," Fiona replied, and it was clear to Jane that the two women truly were very good friends. They were real, genuine friends, not like any of the friends, or supposed friends, that Mildred Collins entertained with such regularity.

She watched Cora Blythe and her nephew leave before she turned her attention to the next of the departing ladies. All in all, it had been a curious night. Interesting, but curious, nonetheless.

"She's rather striking for a maid, isn't she?" Aunt Cora said when their carriage pulled away, and the two of them sat alone. "Young Miss Jane Smith, as you call her."

"Yes, she is rather striking for a maid, Aunt Cora," Edgar said, knowing that it was always best to speak from the heart as far as his aunt was concerned; anything less and she would see through it in a heartbeat.

"I really was so sure that I knew her from somewhere though; there's something so familiar about her. I don't know, perhaps it's that soft light brown hair and those brown, hazily sort of eyes."

"Aunt Cora, I should imagine that half of England has soft light brown hair and those brown, hazily sort of eyes," Edgar said, teasing her gently.

"Edgar!" Cora said and laughed; she adored her nephew, and she liked his cheeky ways.

Edgar was the son of Cora's late brother, a man who had died when Edgar was just a boy of four. He had been orphaned then, for his own mother had died giving birth to him. Cora had wanted to take the boy herself, to raise him as her own, but her father, Edgar's grandfather, had been quite determined to take the boy himself. Between them, they had bestowed all the love and attention that his mother and father would surely have given him had they lived. As a result, Edgar Sinclair, now seventeen years old, had become the most thoughtful, intelligent, and rather amusing young man. Much apart from being her own flesh and blood, Cora realised that she very much liked him as well as she loved him. He was a fine young man, a very deserving young man.

"So, where do you think you know Jane Smith from?" Edgar asked, realising that he was rather keen to talk about the pretty young maid.

"Well, if I knew that, then I wouldn't be racking my brain so hard, would I?" Aunt Cora said, indulging in a little teasing of her own.

"Very good, Aunt. Very good." He chuckled warmly. "I do hope old Morton doesn't give her a rotten time of it because you thought you recognised her," he went on, knowing Morton of old.

"Oh, dear, do you really think he would?" Cora asked, seeming instantly dismayed.

"I find him a very pernicious character, Aunt Cora. Really, I don't know why Fiona keeps him around."

"No, he's not really Fiona's sort of man to have about the house. However, he was Guthrie's butler long before he ever married Fiona. In fact, I do believe he was the butler here when Guthrie was a boy. So, I daresay she has inherited him along with the rest of her husband's belongings."

"Aunt Cora, I don't think I've ever heard you

describe another human being as a belonging! You have quite surprised me."

"I didn't mean it, Edgar. I suppose it's just because I don't like him very much. But no, I didn't mean that! I suppose it all just came out wrong."

"I know, I'm just teasing you. But you're right, there is something about Jane Smith."

"Oh?" Cora said and narrowed those dark eyes of hers. "Is there?"

"Well, I think I find her as intriguing as you do, that's all, Aunt Cora." He was being a little defensive, and he knew it.

"Yes, but I strongly suspect that your interest in her is no doubt very different from mine," Cora said and gave him a mischievous grin.

Despite himself, despite his best attempts to remain stoic, Edgar could feel his cheeks blazing. Really, he was a man; surely, embarrassed blushing was something he had left behind in his youth! But apparently not. So, just what was it about Jane Smith, the young woman he barely knew, which could have such an effect on him?

CHAPTER TWELVE

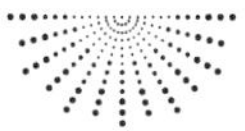

The following week, Jane was working below stairs again. She was in the kitchen, peeling and chopping vegetables and leaving them in bowls of salted cold water ready for the cook to use later in the day. The cook herself was out on the grounds speaking to the gardener about gathering a few nice early autumn apples for a strudel she had it in mind to make for the evening meal. She wanted to make a strudel so big that there would be plenty left for the servants afterwards and she had the full support of Mrs Prescott in doing so. And so it was that Jane had the kitchen to herself for a little while. Betsy was upstairs dusting, the rest of the maids were fully employed, and the footmen were helping Mrs Radcliffe rearrange the furniture in some of the upstairs rooms.

"What have you done with everybody else?" Edgar Sinclair asked, smiling broadly as he strode into the kitchen. "I say, I don't suppose Cook has left any of her wonderful scones lying about unattended, has she?" He looked hopeful, mischievous, and boyish in a very handsome sort of way.

"She counts them, you know," Jane said, smiling and realising just how pleased she was to see him.

He was carrying a book, and it warmed her heart that he had remembered the promise he'd made just nights before at the party. He saw her eyeing the book and smiled.

"I brought this for you," he said and set the book down on the table. She hurriedly dried her hands on a cloth and picked it up. "There's something about you which suggests a simple romance wouldn't keep you entertained, more's the pity," he stated, adding that last with something of a suggestive look. However, it was a look which amused, rather than frightened her. She was certain now that he was not a bit like Franklin Wakefield.

"No, I'm not a very romantic person, sir," Jane said and laughed. She picked up the book and stared at it; It was *Ivanhoe* by Sir Walter Scott.

"This was one of my favourites as a boy. To be honest, it's still a favourite of mine now. It's packed full of adventure; jousts, kidnappings, and what-have-you, but it's all rather thrilling. I suppose it's boyish, but I thought you might like to read a little adventure. I think adventure and excitement in books takes us away from our own world for a while." He looked sad for a moment, and Jane looked straight back down at the book again. Something about the sad look in his beautiful green eyes had taken her aback.

"I can't imagine you needing to escape from your life, sir," Jane said, knowing that it was something of an impertinent assumption but wanting to know a little more about him.

"We all need to escape from our world once in a while, Jane. Although I daresay, I have been more blessed than most."

"I see," she said, seeing nothing. "Well, thank you very much. I swear I will look after it and return it to you as soon as I'm finished." It seemed to her a great privilege to be lent a book that meant so much to its owner. She felt trusted; so trusted that she wished she could tell him everything. At that moment, she wanted to tell him exactly why she was there and how little choice she'd had in the matter. In the end, however, self-preservation prevailed, and she kept quiet.

"What about you, Jane? Where do you come from? Did you go to school or did somebody else teach you to read?" he asked, shifting attention to her and away from himself.

"I was raised in the orphanage in Southwark, sir, and we had to learn to read from the Bible and newspapers. I mean, I am very grateful for that much, but I'd always wished that I might be allowed to read a story now and again."

"I understand that orphanages aren't always the kindest of places," he said, and there it was again, that sadness in his eyes. "And I daresay I ought to think myself very lucky that I wasn't raised in the orphanage, for I was orphaned at four years old, you see," he said, and there it was; the source of his sadness, she was certain of it.

"No, not the kindest of places. Still, I learned to read, and if that is all I ever got from that place, I'm grateful for that much. I'm sorry to hear you were orphaned so young, Mr Sinclair. I suppose you don't have much memory of your mother and father."

"None of my mother, and just a little of my father."

"I don't even know who my parents were," she said with brutal honesty that was gently delivered. "But there are ups and downs in life, aren't there? Like poor Betsy, she remembers her parents well and was raised nicely by them but was never fortunate enough to be taught how to read and write. We all have things to be grateful for and things to feel sad about, I suppose." Jane said and turned the book over and over in her hands. "All of us, I think."

"I do like you, Jane. I find you very interesting, and I'm glad we're friends." He paused and looked into her eyes. "I've made you uncomfortable, haven't I?" he said and winced a little before grinning.

"Not uncomfortable, exactly," Jane said, trying to find the right words to say. "Maybe just a little unsettled. Maybe just a little fearful, although it's not your fault. I suppose what I'm trying to say is that friendships between people of your class and people of mine are not only uncommon but perhaps frowned upon. I really do need this job here, sir, more than you could ever imagine. I wouldn't want to find myself losing my position."

"I would never do anything to hurt you, Jane. I would never do anything to see you out of this position, I promise. We can still be friends though, can't we? Just like this? Just like we are right now?"

"Yes, of course," Jane said and felt suddenly a little tearful; apart from Betsy, she'd never had a friend before.

Betsy was her friend because they shared a room. If Jane was cast out of the house tomorrow, she had little doubt that Betsy would very quickly forget her. That was the nature of things. That was *the way the world worked*, that phrase she had heard far too many times already in life. But Edgar Sinclair was something different; he was seeking out her friendship. They hadn't been thrown together, they didn't work side-by-side. He just liked her for who she was, and it was a very emotional moment for her.

"Are you all right, Jane?"

"Yes," she said and sniffed. "Sorry, I never really had a friend before."

"Then I shall swear right now that we shall be friends forever. There, what do you think of that? Would you mind very much being friends forever with an annoying young man who never stops talking?"

"Yes, I think I would be very glad to be friends forever," Jane said and hurriedly dashed away a tear before it fell.

"I suppose I'd better go before Mrs Prescott comes blustering into the room, hadn't I?" he said, a look in his bright green eyes suggesting that he was hoping she would tell him to stay. She couldn't tell him to stay, he was right. Mrs Prescott might very well bluster into the room at any moment.

"She will come down on me like a ton of bricks if she finds you here, Mr Sinclair," Jane said, wishing she didn't have to send him away.

"All right, I'll go. But first, will you please call me Edgar?"

"I would get into terrible trouble for that," Jane said, her eyes wide with fear.

"Well, just when we're alone, then." He was looking at her hopefully.

"Yes, of course," Jane said, blushing once more as she wondered just when they might be alone again.

"You disappeared for a good long while today, Edgar. I think dear Fiona wondered what had become of you," Cora said as she and her nephew sat down to dinner.

"You mean *you* were wondering what had become of me, Aunt Cora. And if you don't admit it, I shan't tell you a thing," Edgar said, grinning at her as he cut into his veal and ham pie with gusto. "I say, this is really rather good," he said, chewing and speaking all at once. "Oh, sorry, forgive me. Dreadful manners, dreadful boy!" he said and was pleased when his aunt laughed.

"I do like to see you enjoy your food, Edgar. However, if I am honest, I would really rather not see that same food rolling around whilst you speak, and you're right, you are a dreadful boy!" Cora laughed. "Not least because you are trying to divert me from my original intention. So, I shall admit to my own curiosity and ask you to tell me exactly what became of you this afternoon whilst we were supposed to be sitting down to afternoon tea with Fiona Radcliffe."

"You are like a dog with a bone!"

"And you are still trying to put me off."

"All right, I went below stairs to take a book to Jane Smith. She is able to read, but she has no books of her own, so I had promised to lend her one of mine." He kept his eyes on his plate, pleased to note that his voice sounded nonchalant and his cheeks were the normal temperature.

"I see," Cora said as if she wasn't at all surprised to hear exactly who he had darted off to see. "I think you rather like her, don't you? Now I'm, not as old-fashioned in my thinking as most, but you must remember that she is a servant, Edgar. I'm not saying you can't be friends; I'm just advising a little caution. You don't want to go getting her hopes up about the future, it isn't fair."

"Well, you put that very nicely," Edgar said, knowing that his aunt was trying to be kind, knowing that this was the way of things in their world. However, he didn't have to like the way the world worked, did he?

"Don't look like that, my dear. I say this as much for your sake as for hers. You've got a kind heart, a romantic heart I believe, and I don't want to see you get hurt."

"You think that Jane would hurt me, Aunt Cora?"

"No, I don't think so at all. She has a lovely face, that child, and I must admit that there is something about her I rather like, I'm even intrigued by, but that's not really the point I'm trying to make. I don't want you falling in love with somebody that you can't have in the end. I'm not a hard woman, you know that, and with your grandfather's help, I hope we raised you to be kind. In fact, I know we did," she said and looked sad as she always did when she spoke of her father. He had been gone almost a year, and they both missed him still so very much. "But I still have to bear in mind what it was that your mother and father would have wanted for you. My dear Edgar, I don't think my brother would have been at all pleased by the idea of you setting your sights on one of Fiona Radcliffe's maids."

"I don't think I'm setting my sights on her, Aunt Cora," Edgar said, reacting instantly but knowing that his words weren't entirely the truth. "There's nothing wrong with being friends, is there?"

"No, nothing at all," Cora said, and he could see that she didn't look at all convinced. "Tell me, which of your books did you lend her?"

"Ivanhoe," he said, and he saw his aunt's face change. "What? What's the matter with that?"

"You've loved that book for so many years, you've read it time and time again. I do believe there isn't a book you prefer in all the world. Forgive me if I'm wrong, but I judge it to be rather an intimate thing to lend your most treasured book to somebody. Edgar, do be careful," she said and smiled at him warmly.

"I suppose I like her because we have so much in common. You might think that unusual, given our respective statuses in society, but there is a very fundamental condition of life which we have shared."

“And that is?” Cora asked gently.

“That we were both orphaned. I mean, I know our fortunes from that moment certainly divide us. I was fortunate enough to have a grandfather to raise me, and I always have you in my life, Aunt Cora. Poor Jane Smith wasn’t quite so lucky, having no idea who her parents were at all and having been orphaned from birth. I suppose at least I have some little memory of my father up until I was four years old. Spending time with Jane makes me more grateful for what I did have rather than mournful for what I lost.”

“The poor girl,” Cora said and abruptly put her knife and fork down. “An orphanage, you say?” She was looking at him most intently.

“Yes, that’s right.”

“In London?” Although her questioning made an attempt at idle curiosity, Edgar was certain that there was something more determined behind it.

“Yes, in London. Southwark, as a matter of fact.”

“Southwark?” Cora said, and suddenly the colour drained from her face.

"Aunt Cora? Are you quite all right? My dear woman, you look most dreadfully pale. What is it?" Edgar said, and he was so concerned that he set down his own knife and fork and raced around the table to take a seat by her side. He picked up her hand and held onto it. "Aunt Cora?"

"Forgive me, Edgar, I do feel a little peculiar."

"What can I do to help?"

"I need to go back to Fiona's house, Edgar."

"To Fiona's house?" he asked, utterly confused.

"Yes, there's something I need to enquire about."

"Is it urgent, Aunt Cora? I ask only because of the lateness of the hour. Perhaps it would be better for us to go tomorrow. I wouldn't really want to take you out tonight when you look so dreadfully pale. Can I convince you to delay?"

"Yes, of course," Cora said and let out a great puff of air. "Forgive me, I think I was being a little silly. My dear Edgar, it's nothing important, just a whim. I won't make a fool of myself by telling you all about it, I shall just wait until tomorrow and have a few words with Fiona."

"Are you sure?" Edgar asked, not at all convinced.

"Yes, I'm sure. In fact, we shan't go until the afternoon. There, do you see? It really isn't urgent."

"As you wish," Edgar said and got to his feet the moment his aunt picked up her knife and fork again.

However, as he retook his own seat and set about his meal, Edgar had the sense that there really was a story to be told.

CHAPTER THIRTEEN

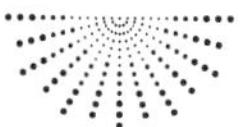

"I reckon you've been getting too comfortable in that place, girl," Harry Newland said as the two of them stood in that very same alleyway just off the market in Covent Garden. "I bet, after all these weeks, you thought I'd never come back. Well, I'm just a man who knows how to bide his time, that's all."

"I know I'm not with Mrs Prescott today, but I won't be able to linger here long, Harry. She really is watching me like a hawk all the time, and if I'm ten minutes late, she'll be out looking for me. Not that I mind, of course, it's just that I know you want me to keep a job there," she added the last pointedly and saw the look of annoyance on his face.

"Yes, all right. All right!" he said and shook his head in exasperation. "Well, I'll get right to the point. After all my watching and waiting, I've decided that night-time is the best time to set my little devils loose in your mistress' house. I've seen far too many servants coming and going all day long to manage it in the daytime, so you're going to have to find a way to creep out and meet me."

"All right," Jane said, feeling so sickened that it was almost as if she had been punched in the stomach. How she had hoped and prayed that this day would never come. "When?"

"Friday night. That gives you three days to figure out how you're going to safely get out of the house and meet me. Now then, I'll get as close to the property as possible, but I won't go on it. I don't want to get caught trespassing, you see, that comes with a little time behind bars these days," he said, and once again Jane was reminded of his monumental selfishness. Night after night, he sent little children out to trespass when he wouldn't so much as put a toe on somebody's property himself in case a peeler walked by.

"Where then?" Jane asked, feeling utterly nauseous.

"Just come out onto the street from the servants' entrance and turn left. Only a hundred yards or so from there you'll find one of those little pocket parks that the posh folk like so much. I'll be waiting in there for you from midnight onwards."

"I can't guarantee that I'll be able to get there exactly at midnight, Harry, not without being caught."

"I will wait there until you arrive. You're not getting out of this, Jane Ashford. Just you make sure you turn up on Friday night otherwise my next stop will be the nearest police station, got it?"

"Yes."

"And your next stop will be the gallows, girl," he went on.

"Yes, I said I understood, didn't I?" Jane said angrily. "Now, I'd better get back, hadn't I?"

"I'll see you Friday," Harry said, his voice alone a threat.

As Jane walked away, tears streamed down her face. She had been working for Fiona Radcliffe for almost four months now, and just as Harry had said, she had grown a little too comfortable there.

Despite Mrs Prescott and Mr Morton, she liked it. She liked the work, the house, and most of all, she liked Edgar Sinclair. He'd promised to be her friend forever, but if he knew all that there was to know about her, he would turn his back in an instant. If he knew of the plan she was such a great part of, he would surely despise her. And if he knew exactly what it was Harry Newland had hanging over her head as a bribe, a fine young man like Edgar Sinclair would be quite rightly appalled by her.

Perhaps the tiny slice of joy that she had silently prayed for had been delivered. Now that she'd experienced it in the form of that tentative friendship, Jane almost wished she'd never prayed for it in the first place. She was about to have to give everything up; she was on the verge of losing Edgar Sinclair's friendship forever. Why, oh, why, did life have to be so full of heartbreak?

"What took you so long? I was expecting you back ten minutes ago!" Mrs Prescott said unreasonably the very moment Jane walked back in through the servant's entrance.

"I was trying to get the spices a little cheaper as you'd asked me to do, Mrs Prescot. The costermonger was really very awkward, and it took me longer than expected," she said, knowing full well that it was an untruth. The costermonger who sold spices much preferred Jane to Mrs Prescott and had given her a few pennies off the price without arguing. Still, she had to explain her absence somehow. "I did get them a little cheaper in the end," she added, hoping to give herself some credibility.

"Never mind that now. The mistress wants to see you right away!" Mrs Prescott said in a voice which suggested that Jane was in some kind of trouble.

"The mistress? But what about?" Jane asked, setting down the woven basket on the large kitchen table and feeling her heart begin to pick up the pace.

"Well, how should I know what it's about? You'd better get yourself up to the drawing room quick smart, or you'll be in even more trouble," Mrs Prescott said with an unkind glimmer of glee in her eyes.

"I'm in trouble?" Jane was racking her brain; had somebody seen her talking to Harry Newland and already reported it to Fiona Radcliffe? Surely not! Surely there hadn't been time!

"How should I know?" Mrs Prescott said again, and Jane realised that hateful old woman was simply trying to unnerve her before she even made her way to the drawing room. Of course, there was nothing to say that she was not in trouble, though, was there? "Now, get going, I've already had to put Mrs Radcliffe off once!"

Without another word, Jane darted out of the kitchen. She hurried up the servants' staircase and along to the drawing room. She paused outside the door for a moment or two to straighten her dress and slow her ragged breathing. Once she was satisfied with her general appearance, she tapped timidly on the heavy oak door. She opened it and cautiously walked inside.

"Mrs Prescott said you wished to see me, Mrs

Radcliffe?" she said in a tiny voice, somewhat horrified to see that Cora Blythe was also in the room.

The two women were sitting side-by-side on the couch nearest to the fireplace, and Jane had an awful feeling that she knew what was coming. Jane was absolutely certain that Cora Blythe had discovered something of the tentative friendship between her nephew and Jane, and no doubt she had come to reprimand her for it. The very idea that the woman would think her nothing more than a rough little maid who was looking for an easy time of it embarrassed Jane before a word had even been spoken. Her cheeks were already violently scarlet and her eyes swimming with the tears which threatened to fall.

"Come in, my dear," Fiona Radcliffe said, beckoning her further into the room. "Please don't look so worried, it isn't anything you've done wrong," she went on, and seeing her smile of warmth, Jane could have cried with relief.

"It really is my fault, Jane," Cora Blythe, smiling as warmly as Fiona Radcliffe, began to speak. "What I mean is, it was really I who wanted to speak to you. I do hope you don't mind."

"No, Ma'am, I don't mind at all," Jane said, her confusion draining her to the point of exhaustion.

"The thing is, my nephew, Edgar, he mentioned to me that you had been raised in the orphanage in Southwark," Mrs Blythe began awkwardly.

"Yes, Ma'am."

"You really are going to think this a most peculiar thing, and I must apologise entirely if I am wrong. The thing is, my dear, I was so certain that we had met before when I first saw you here on the night of the party. The night when you were kind enough to help me back into my cloak," she said, looking almost as nervous as Jane felt. "You were so familiar to me, my dear, that I haven't quite been able to get you out of my mind ever since. Do you mind if I tell you a story?"

"No, not at all," Jane said, and now didn't know what to think or feel; this was all so peculiar.

"My dear, you are probably already well aware that I am a widow. My dear husband, Malcolm Blythe, died some years ago now. He had something on his mind, you see, and I do believe that his broken heart shortened his life. You see, some years before he had lost his sister. Her name was Catherine, and she was a good deal younger than Malcolm. She was one of those late babies that comes as a surprise to everybody, I suppose. Anyway, about sixteen years ago, perhaps a little longer, Catherine fell in love." Cora Blythe paused for such a long time that Jane realised that the poor woman had been overcome with emotion.

"Take your time, my dear," Mrs Radcliffe interjected, taking Cora's hand and patting it encouragingly.

"Do forgive me," Cora said before continuing. "Yes, little Catherine fell in love. She was so very young herself, only just seventeen. Anyway, with their own parents long gone, Malcolm was her guardian, as her only brother, you understand."

"I see," Jane said and nodded kindly.

"We had already been married for some time by then and had never been blessed with children of our own. I suppose we both saw her as sort of a daughter to us, really. Anyway, Malcolm very much objected to the young man that Catherine had fallen in love with. He was a decent sort of a chap, and he'd come from what used to be a fine family. However, they had fallen on hard times, extraordinary hard times, and Malcolm could see that there was no way back for them. He didn't want Catherine to live a life of poverty." She paused and took a sip of what Jane thought might well be cold tea.

"He thought it was just a phase, a young girl's fancy. The young man was a romantic sort, very goodhearted, always sending her poems that he'd written. I suppose it was on account of that that my poor dear Malcolm thought Catherine had simply been easily swayed and would be just as easily swayed by a man of better means if he kept the two of them apart. It was a mistake he never forgave himself for," she said and reached into the sleeve of her immaculate dark blue dress to retrieve a white cotton handkerchief. She dabbed her eyes as Fiona continued to hold tightly to her hand.

"You're a clever young woman, so my nephew tells me, and I'm certain you have already perceived that my husband's young sister ran away so that she could be with the man she loved. She was some years from the age of majority, and so she knew that the only way she could be with the man she loved was to elope and marry him. And that's just what she did."

"Your husband must have been very sad, Mrs Blythe," Jane said, feeling that she ought to say something.

"You really are so very kind, my dear. Those eyes, those wonderful hazel brown eyes of yours," Cora Blythe said and stared at her for a moment, studying her. "He was proud and silly like most men and, at first, he refused to have anything further to do with her. He was an old-fashioned sort of a man, and he had declared more than once that she had made her bed and she must lay in it. I did what I could to keep track of her, I really did love her so very much, you see. The couple lived in Southwark, south of the river and in the most dreadful circumstances. I called in upon them once or twice, having to lie to my dear Malcolm in order to do so. I even tried to give Catherine a little money, but she was so like her brother in that regard; so very proud and determined. But she was so lovely."

"Take a breath, my dear," Fiona Radcliffe said. "And Jane, forgive me, I should have asked you to sit down.

Please," Mrs Radcliffe held out her hand to indicate the couch opposite.

"Thank you, Ma'am," Jane said and sat down a little awkwardly.

"Of course, Malcolm found out all about it. I blame myself really, for what happened next, because he was so furious, you see. I'd lied to him, and he took it as a betrayal. As I said, a little too proud for his own good. Anyway, he forbade me to ever see her again, and I knew that I would have to stay away from Southwark for a good long while. You see, I thought we had time to wait it out, I thought Malcolm would soon give in, and the relationship would be repaired. However, everything took a lot longer than I expected. Malcolm indulged his pride, and in the end, he paid a terrible price for it." Once again, she dabbed at her eyes.

"More than five years passed before Malcolm decided that he missed his beloved sister, and it was time to extend an olive branch. Unfortunately, it was all too late. I took him to the house where Catherine and her husband had lived, but there was another family there. They were no help, of course, telling me that they had no idea of the previous occupants, nor even could they provide proper details for the landlord. We tracked him down in the end, of course, but more and more time was passing. Eventually, we discovered that Catherine had died three years before. The poor child, she had been only just nineteen when she passed away. Her husband hadn't outlived her by long, both of them easily succumbing to the maladies of poverty so much quicker than others in their position might have."

"I'm so sorry, Mrs Blythe," Jane said, feeling a lump in her throat and a pain in her heart; why was this so very upsetting? It was sad, of course, but what had it to do with Jane? Why did she feel it so deeply?

"The landlord told us that there had been a child, a baby girl, but he had no real idea what had become of her. He was certain that she had gone to family, presumably Catherine's husband's family. We couldn't track them down, however, because they had moved out of London in hopes of appealing to wealthier relatives in the North. Even now, I couldn't tell you what became of that family."

"And they took the little girl with them? The baby?" Jane asked, her voice cracking and her throat dry.

"When Edgar told me that you'd been raised in an orphanage in Southwark, I finally realised why it was that you are so familiar to me. I really don't know why I didn't see it immediately. I suppose I can only explain it by saying that my heart was likely protecting itself. You see, my dear, you are the absolute image of Catherine Blythe. Well, not really Catherine Blythe, but Catherine Ash...."

"Ashford?" Jane said and began to shake from head to foot, the colour draining out of her face.

"Yes, Ashford. I was discouraged at first, knowing that your name is Smith. But still, my dear Edgar took me to the orphanage this morning before I came here, I was so determined, you see. When they told me that they had never raised a child called Jane Smith in the last years, I was disappointed. And then I asked if there was perhaps a child by the name of Ashford, and they kindly told me that, almost 2 and a half years ago, a girl by the name of Jane Ashford was taken by a family in Regent's Park to be employed as a household servant." Cora's tears were rolling down her face now unchecked, as were Jane's. "What is your name, my dear?"

"I am Jane Ashford," Jane said and all but dissolved

into sobs. "And I'm telling the truth, Mrs Blythe, really. I'm sure, if you took me to the orphanage in Southwark now, they would be able to identify me easily."

"There is no need to do that, Jane, I know who you are. From the very moment that Edgar told me you had been raised in an orphanage in Southwark, I knew. I haven't slept a wink, truly; in fact, I almost came back to you last night."

"I haven't been able to go by my own name because... because..." Jane said, realising at that moment, just how cruel life was. She had found family at last, real family who would care for her and soothe the struggles of her past. But she had found them too late, far too late. She had changed, she had killed a man, and she had set Fiona Radcliffe up to have her house overrun with vermin. As kind and caring as Cora Blythe was, Jane couldn't imagine that such information would see her open her arms to her husband's niece. Jane let the tears fall.

"There, there, my dear," Cora said and moved to sit beside her on the couch, putting her arms around her and rocking her gently back and forth.

After some time and two hot, sweet cups of tea, Jane had begun to recover. She knew she couldn't move into a new life holding onto the secrets of the old one, and so the time had come to at least tell the two women why she was there.

"I haven't had a very good time of it since leaving the orphanage, Mrs Blythe," Jane began, fearful of the consequences.

"Please, do call me Aunt Cora," Cora said, her arm still around her.

"You might not want that... let me speak first."

"Of course, but I understand."

Jane swallowed, how could she tell them of her shame. "I wasn't at all happy in Regent's Park. Mr and Mrs Collins weren't very nice people."

"Oh, goodness, no, they are absolutely ghastly!" Cora said and started to laugh.

"You know them?"

"Enough to give them a very wide berth," Cora said and nodded for her to continue.

"Whilst I was working in their house, at a party, I met another maid, a lady's maid, called Maud Parsons. She told me that she knew of a man who was looking for a housekeeper and she convinced me that the grass was greener elsewhere."

"But it wasn't?" Fiona Radcliffe said, leaning forward in her own seat, absolutely mesmerised by the unfolding drama.

"No, it wasn't. The man drove me away from Regent's Park, and we were supposed to be going to his house in Camden Town. But he drove me down to Southwark, to an awful rotten old tavern and he expected me to... he wanted me to... there was this dreadful man, you see, and I was thrown down on a bed in a horrible little room..." She was so humiliated, she couldn't finish.

"Oh, my poor child," Cora said, and tears rolled down her face once again.

"I escaped before anything happened, but I found myself alone on the streets. I had no references, nothing, not even my possessions." Jane realised she had neglected to tell her aunt that she had only escaped by killing a man. She just couldn't find the right words. "I was given shelter by a man called Harry Newland. He's a rat catcher, but he is not an honest man. He has a basement full of poor, desperate little children, and he makes them sneak into people's homes at night to release the rats he keeps in cages. It is his way of getting work from the best houses in London so that he can make more money."

"As dreadful as that is, it's hardly your fault, Jane." Cora was stroking her hair now; it was so wonderfully soothing.

"The thing is, it was Harry Newland who made me come here to look for work. I'm too big to crawl through windows to release rats, you see, and he was aware that Mrs Radcliffe always makes sure that everything is locked up tight around the house at night time." She turned to look at Fiona Radcliffe. "I really am so very sorry. Harry Newland told me that I would have to work here and get your trust and then, finally, he would give me a bag of rats to release in the dead of night. I was so afraid of him, truly afraid, but I know that is no excuse. I shouldn't have done it, I shouldn't be here, and I really am so very sorry." Once again, Jane was sobbing.

"As much as I detest rats, Jane, I detest rotten, predatory men like this Harry Newland even more. I have heard your story, and I cannot imagine how terribly alone you must have felt since leaving the orphanage. The truth is, I imagine that you felt terribly alone when you were there in the first place, and I cannot begin to imagine how I would have survived in your position. I do not blame you, Jane, and you are in no trouble with me. I am just glad that you and Cora have found one another at last, after all these years. I know how the loss of your mother broke Cora's heart, and when she discovered that there had been a baby and there was no sign of her, her heart was broken afresh. Your being here now is like a miracle, a true miracle. Although I must ask you, my dear girl, are their rats loose in my house currently?" Fiona Radcliffe finished her wonderful speech with a wince.

"Oh no, Mrs Radcliffe, Harry hasn't brought the rats to me yet. And of course, I won't do it now. I shall just leave; I'll run and hide from him. I'm so sorry, Mrs Radcliffe, you were so kind to take me on in the first place, and I really have enjoyed working here. I know I've been deceitful, and it's kind of you to be so understanding, I wonder if you would write me a reference so that I might find work somewhere else," Jane said, the very thought of leaving almost breaking her heart.

"So you can work as a servant?" Cora said in an amusingly booming and scandalised voice. "No, no, my dear! There'll be none of that, will there, Fiona?"

"No, of course not," Fiona said and laughed.

"You will be coming to live with me, of course. You are my husband's niece and, whilst we are not related by blood, you are as much my niece, in my opinion. I have never been blessed with children of my own, but I count myself very fortunate to have Edgar and now you. No, your days of being bossed around by the likes of Mrs Prescott are over, my dear."

"But what about Harry Newland? He really is a frightening man," Jane said, fearing that Harry would not only find the nearest peeler and tell him where she was but that he might also do something to hurt Fiona Radcliffe. He was vindictive, and he would undoubtedly be furious after having put in what he saw as so much work.

"When are you to take the rats from him?" Fiona asked and thoughtfully chewed her bottom lip.

"On Friday night after midnight. I am to meet him in the little pocket park further along the street."

"Then you should," Fiona said and suddenly looked pleased with herself. "And we shall have some policemen standing by ready to take Harry Newland into custody!"

"Oh, how wonderfully devious of you, Fiona!" Cora said, thrilled and a little excited by the whole thing. "Glorious! You have come up with a very clever way of giving that dreadful man a taste of his own medicine. Well done, Fiona, well done indeed!" She turned to look at Jane. "I'm afraid you must maintain the appearance of a maid for the next few days then, my dear. We can't have him suspecting something and not turning up at the appointed hour. You don't mind very much, do you?"

"No, I don't mind at all," Jane said, swept along by the tide of it all.

"Don't look so worried, my dear, there will be enough policemen there; nothing will happen, no harm will come to you." Fiona was smiling at her.

"Of course," Jane said and nodded, smiling with as much confidence as she could muster.

If only those two fine women knew that to catch Harry Newland would be the beginning of the end for Jane Ashford.

CHAPTER FOURTEEN

"I thought I might find you here," Edgar said with a grin when he bounded into the kitchen.

"Where else would I be but peeling potatoes?" Jane said and smiled. Although Edgar didn't know it, this would be her last day with him, and she wasn't going to waste a moment of it being shy or embarrassed.

"So, it looks like we share an aunt, doesn't it?"

"Yes, I suppose we're cousins."

"Not really, Jane," he said and stared right into her eyes. "I mean we're not related by blood, are we? But

I am pleased we're going to be living in the same house."

"I think you seem pleased that we're not related, Edgar," Jane said and felt a little hurt.

"Ah, you think I wouldn't want to be related to an orphan girl who works in service when she's not working for the rat catcher?" he asked, and his grin became mischievous. "No, that's not the reason I'm glad we're not related, but I'll leave it to you to work that out."

"I'm not looking forward to tonight," Jane said truthfully. She had decided to unpack his other words later and study them properly. Not that it mattered, of course, for neither Edgar nor Cora would want to know a thing about her once they found out that she had killed Franklin Wakefield.

"I'm not surprised, this Harry Newland character sounds rather a rough sort. I can't bear to think of the things you've suffered over the years, Jane. We were both orphans, and yet I was treated well, raised in privilege, and you weren't. It hurts my heart; I hope you know."

"There isn't anything that either one of us could have done about that, Edgar. Even now," she said and shrugged. "Even now, this is just life and life means being at the mercy of whatever happens next. I am not yet fifteen, and I'm sure that you aren't very much older. What say do we have in any of it?" she stated and stared a little vacantly into the distance, unaware for some moments that he was studying her with great curiosity.

"I do believe you're a great thinker, Jane. From now on, let's make a pact; you do all the thinking, and I'll do all the idling. What do you say?" He was trying to cheer her up, she knew he was.

"I say that sounds like a very good idea," she said and laughed, partly amused, partly determined to show a little gratitude for the effort he was putting in.

"Are you very worried about tonight?"

"Yes, I am." She really was worried, but not for the reasons Edgar likely assumed. She wasn't afraid of Harry Newland; she was afraid of how he was about to destroy her new-found life.

"Well, don't be. I'll be there with you," he said,

partially whispering as if his aunt might be standing behind him.

"You can't be there, Edgar. As soon as Harry sees me with you or anybody else, he will take to his heels, and he won't be caught. No, I have to walk down into that park alone, Edgar."

"I didn't mean I'd be striding along at your side for all to see!" Edgar laughed, his green eyes a little excited as if this was all some great adventure. If only he knew the truth, he wouldn't be excited; he would be disgusted. "No, I mean to set off much, much earlier. I mean to be hiding in the bushes in the pocket park long before Harry Newland even arrives. I know there will be policemen in the area, probably even some hiding in the park too, but I want to be there. I think I want you to know that I'm there, ready to rush in if anything happens."

"That's very kind of you, Edgar, but as you said yourself, there will be peelers... *policemen* there," she said, beginning to feel a little embarrassed about the way she spoke now, even if it wasn't quite as rough as most. How could she be a part of this family and still use the parlance of the street?

Of course, Jane knew that there was little point in letting go of her world of peelers, rat catchers, and half-starved children. She wasn't related to Cora Blythe nor Edgar Sinclair by blood, and even if she was, they would be unlikely to own up to any connection with her once the truth was known. So, *peelers* it was!

"Well, I will be there before the peelers. I will be waiting in the bushes no matter what you say, Jane Ashford!" he said and grinned at her, his use of her real name, giving her the strangest feeling. "Well, I suppose I'd better make myself scarce before our favourite harridan comes bounding into the room to terrify us both. Perhaps we ought to send her to deal with Harry Newland? I think she'd do rather well."

"I think so," Jane said and laughed, trying to hold down her sadness; this would be the last time they were ever alone together; she knew it.

"Well, until tonight!" Edgar said and, hearing footsteps approaching, he darted right out of the servants' entrance and away into the grounds.

It was well after midnight by the time Jane made her way along the moonlit street to the pocket park just a few hundred yards away. The night was absolutely silent, so silent that she felt entirely alone. But the police sergeant who had turned up at the house and talked her through it all as Cora and Fiona sat holding her hands, had promised her that the park would be full of waiting peelers. And, of course, Edgar Sinclair, if he hadn't already been discovered by an eagle-eyed policeman and sent on his way.

Jane reached the park and pushed open the wide wrought iron gate, the squeak that the hinges made seeming to pierce the darkness louder than a shout. She let the gate close behind her and slowly wandered into the dark and secluded little park. The trees and shrubs seemed to make it darker, the silvery moonlight held back behind so many leafy obstructions. However, now that she was in the park, Jane could sense the presence of others. She only hoped that Harry was here so that this whole dreadful thing could be done. She needed to get him out of her life, to be certain that Fiona Radcliffe would be safe. However much Fiona and Cora would resent her, *despise her*, in the future, she owed them both that.

"Good, you're here," Harry's voice, even whispered, was unmistakable. Where he must've crept up on her from was a mystery to her, he was slinkier and stealthier than any one of his rats. "Now then, I don't want to linger long here. Did anyone see you coming out?" he asked, an edge to his voice which suggested a little nervousness.

How she despised him; he didn't care about tiny children taking all the risks for him, but when it came to taking any for himself, he was a shambles. Despicable man!

"No, nobody," she said, wondering how long the peelers would leave it before they raced out and grabbed their man.

"Right, take this sack," he said, handing her an extraordinarily heavy sack of rats. It turned her stomach to take the bag, for it leaned against her leg and she could feel the warm little bodies through the canvas tumbling over one another, waiting for their chance to infest Fiona Radcliffe's home. "There's a few more than usual, but I want to get this one right first time. What we need, girl, is a right good infestation!" he said, his voice rising above the whisper in his excitement; the prospect of fortunes to come.

Before she could respond, Harry cried out. Two large hands had gripped his shoulders from behind, and suddenly there was a swarm of peelers all around him, taking him down to the floor and subduing him.

"I know this was you! I know you did this, you treacherous little ingrate!" Harry screamed from beneath the blanket of peelers. "I'll make you pay for this; you know I will!"

Jane began to back away, not wanting to hear him shout her sins aloud. However, she backed right into somebody and cried out herself, until she turned, and broad arms wrapped themselves around her. It was Edgar, he had waited there for her just as he'd promised. She leaned her forehead onto his chest and began to weep.

"There, there, Jane, it's all over now," Edgar said in a soothing tone as he stroked her soft brown hair.

If only he had known that that was exactly why she was crying; it really was all over now.

CHAPTER FIFTEEN

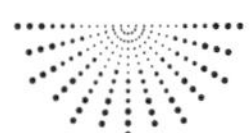

"Drink it down, it will steady your nerves, child," Cora was fussing about her like a mother hen.

"Thank you," Jane said, hating the taste of the brandy but not wanting to turn away the kindness of Cora Blythe. She drank it down quickly, coughing as the fiery liquid burned her throat.

"Better?" Cora said, smiling, and Jane simply coughed in response, her eyes bulging.

"Yes," she croaked, and Edgar began to laugh.

"She did so well, Aunt Cora," he said, wincing when

his aunt turned to give him a look that was as fiery as the brandy.

"It really was naughty of you, Edgar," Fiona Radcliffe said, shaking her head but smiling at him indulgently. "If something had happened to you, your aunt would have been beside herself."

"And if something had happened to Jane, I would have been beside *myself*," Edgar retorted, and Fiona spread her hands wide, clearly having no response but smiling at him.

"Very well, very well, but it was difficult enough for me to know this little one was out there. It really would have added to things if I'd known, Edgar. The two of you are the only family I have, barring my dear Fiona, and I wouldn't be at all pleased to have to let either one of you go."

"I think you're going to have to let me go," Jane said, the words spilling out of her seemingly of their own volition; the time was now, the time had come.

"Let you go? No, I won't hear any of that. You are my husband's niece, my dear Catherine's baby girl, and I shan't let you out of my sight." Cora was most vehement.

"Tonight, Harry Newland is going to tell something to the police that will very likely see me taken to the gallows, Mrs Blythe. It is the very thing he held over my head to have me come here in the first place and try to do Mrs Ratcliffe such a terrible wrong with the rats." Jane kept her eyes on Cora; she couldn't look at Fiona, and she most certainly couldn't look at Edgar. The room fell silent.

"What on earth are you talking about, Jane?" Cora asked after some moments of silence.

"I killed a man," Jane said, getting right to the heart of it. "He was a wicked and deceitful man, but he was a human being, and I killed him."

"I'm sure there was a good reason for it," Edgar said, flying to her defence before he even knew any of the details. Such a reaction made her feel cared for, truly cared for, for the first time in her life. It was unconditional; it didn't matter to Edgar the circumstances; he had instinctively decided to be on her side no matter what.

"Edgar, let Jane tell it," Fiona said in a gentle and reasonable voice. "Jane, you must tell us everything," she went on, sitting down by her side and taking her hand. She was flanked by Fiona and Cora, the only two women who had shown her an ounce of true maternal feeling in her life.

"I told you I had escaped from the man who had taken me from the Collins' house in Regent's Park, the man who had promised me work as a housekeeper. He had taken me to the Dog and Duck Tavern in Southwark and forced me into a room upstairs. The landlord of the Dog and Duck was the first man he was giving me to, and he waited outside the room whilst the landlord tried to..." She paused for a moment. "Anyway, the landlord was drunk and unsteady on his feet, so I raced over to him and pushed him over. He was a big man, but so drunk that his balance was all but gone. I was so terrified, I couldn't bear the idea of what was about to happen to me, so I just ran. But Mr Wakefield was there at the top of the stairs, he was blocking my way. I was so determined to get out that I pushed past him, or at least I tried to, but he fell back down the stairs. He fell from top to bottom and lay dead. That was when I ran, may God forgive me. I jumped over his dead body, and I ran away. I ran right into a little girl who innocently offered me a place to hide. However, it was Harry Newland's lair, and I was in such a state that I told him what I'd done. He knew who I'd killed, he knew how I'd killed him, and he threatened to go to the police. I suppose I've always known that I would end up on the gallows' steps sooner or later, and now I wish it had been sooner. I can't bear that I've found such kind people who care for me and now I have to tell them this; now I have to tell you all what a dreadful person I am."

"There, just as I said! There wasn't a thing you could have done about it, Jane. And you didn't push him to his death, you were just trying to escape, that's all. We'll go to the peelers ourselves, and we'll tell them just exactly what happened." Edgar said, almost desperate in his need to protect her.

"The *peelers,* Edgar?" Cora said and, quite unbelievably, chuckled. "Jane, my dear, this Mr Wakefield; I presume you are talking of Mr Franklin Wakefield of Camden Town?" she said, a smile spreading across her face.

"Yes, Mr Franklin Wakefield. That was the man who lied to me, that was the man who tricked me."

"Well, unless you have murdered him in the last two days, I do believe that he is not the only person who has tricked you, my dear," Cora said and put an arm around her, pulling her in close. "Jane, my poor girl, I have seen Franklin Wakefield this week, although not through choice. The detestable man was in attendance at my regular bridge game in Camden Town. There is something about him I've never liked, so I have never invited him to my own home or willingly spent time in his company. However, in this part of London, crossing paths is unavoidable," Cora said, wandering into a whole different conversation.

"He's alive?" Jane said, feeling almost faint. "You are certain, Mrs Blythe? Forgive me, but I pushed Franklin Wakefield clean down the steps of the Dog and Duck, and there he lay at the bottom."

"And how long ago was this?" Edgar asked, kneeling in front of her.

"Almost ten months ago now, I suppose. Yes, about ten months."

"Ah, so, it would seem he didn't trip down the stone steps coming out of his club in Mayfair then!" Cora said and gave a most unladylike snort. "Of course, he couldn't admit to how it really had happened, could he?"

"He was hurt then?" Jane said, still dumbfounded.

"A little, nothing life-changing," Cora said and shrugged. "He hobbled along with a walking stick for a couple of weeks, nothing more than that. Although now that I know what a dreadful man he is, it would have served him right if he really had expired at the bottom of the stairs in the Dog and Duck."

"Cora!" Fiona said, her hand flying to her chest.

"Well, what a vile creature!"

"I agree, Aunt Cora," Edgar said, looking furious.

"That wouldn't have done Jane any good though, would it?" Fiona said sensibly.

"No, it wouldn't." Cora nodded. "But who did you say was the woman who arranged all of this?" Cora looked at her curiously. "A maid, wasn't it?"

"Yes, Miss Emma Talbot's lady's maid. Her name is Maud Parsons." Jane could hardly keep the bile from her voice when she thought of what the dreadful

Maud Parsons, *no better than she ought to be*, had put her through.

"Oh, the one with the ringlets and the straight back?" Cora asked and looked at Fiona. "Do you remember her? The Christmas event last year, Fiona? That saucy little thing who strutted about as if she owned the place!"

"Oh, yes, Lord Talbot's Christmas ball, I remember it well," Fiona said, nodding. "There was something about that young woman that I couldn't quite put my finger on."

"Well, now you can," Cora said and raised her eyebrows.

"Lord Talbot?" Jane said inquisitively.

"Yes, he's Emma Talbot's father. A baron, which is why she always trots about with a lady's maid. Emma is a pleasant enough young woman, but perhaps a little vain. Anyway, her vanity dictates she has maids who always looks rather fashionable, and this is the result. Well, I shall be writing to her and, if I have no joy, I shall be writing to her father," Cora said, becoming annoyed, maternal, and protective.

"Mrs Blythe, I really wouldn't want anybody to know what my life has been like, I wouldn't want it to be so public," Jane said, knowing that she was in no position to expect anything. She had already been spared the gallows, should she not just be glad about that?

"Of course, of course. Well, perhaps just writing to her is enough. I'm sure neither Emma Talbot nor her father would be keen to have any of this known, and as for Franklin Wakefield, I don't think he would either. However, I want it to be known that neither one of them is to come near you again. I want Franklin Wakefield to know that I am watching him, that his days of tricking young servant girls so terribly are over. It will all be done very secretively, Jane, but you must understand I couldn't bear the idea of this happening to somebody else." Cora seemed firm, and Jane knew it made sense. She couldn't bear for it to happen to anybody else either.

"So, now this is all decided, let's talk about something a bit more cheerful, shall we?" Edgar said, still kneeling on the rug in front of her. She felt surrounded by care, such warm care she almost cried. "Let's talk about the wonderful life Jane is going to have when she comes to live with us, Aunt Cora."

"Yes, let's talk about that!" Cora said and beamed brightly, turning to look at Jane. "Oh, yes, my dear girl, I'm going to look after you. You might not have had the best start in life, but I will make up for that. I will do just what I should have been doing all these years; taking care of my husband's dear little niece."

So, Jane really had found a family at last. They might not be blood kin, but they were her family, nonetheless.

CHAPTER SIXTEEN

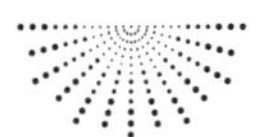

Ever since Jane's connection to Cora Blythe had been made known in Fiona Radcliffe's house, Mrs Prescott and Mr Mason had been silently beside themselves. They hated the idea of a servant being suddenly raised up, curiously snobbish in that perverse way that was peculiar to the working classes. They hated their position, but the idea that they were as good as anybody else was too much for them to cope with. Still, that wasn't going to be Jane's concern for very much longer.

Whilst Cora had been busy making preparations for Jane to move into her home on the other side of Covent Garden, she had continued to stay with Fiona. Of course, now she slept above stairs rather than below, and she took her meals with Fiona every day. Cora visited every day, and Edgar turned up with greater regularity than normal. It was as if a whole new world was being opened to her, and Jane could hardly believe her luck.

More than once, she had been tempted to think about the past, so much so that she had realised, inevitably, that had she not been so cruelly treated by Maud Parsons and Franklin Wakefield in the beginning, she would never have found herself thrown onto the path of the dreadful Harry Newland. And without Harry, she would never have worked in Fiona's house and met the wonderful, kindly wife of her maternal uncle. Fate was a funny thing, wasn't it?

"You really don't need to go to so much trouble, Mrs Ratcliffe," Jane said, feeling a little embarrassed but excited nonetheless; she'd certainly never thought that a party would ever be held in her honour.

"It's been so exciting, not to mention the fact that you worked as a servant in this house and I feel I must do something to redress the balance. And in any case, I shall miss having you here, and I want to say goodbye properly."

"Mrs Radcliffe, I'm sure I will see you several times a week, just as Cora does," Jane said, but couldn't hold back her smile; how wonderful to even *be* at a party, never mind be the very *reason* for it.

"I know, I know, but I should like to have a party for you, nonetheless. Cora and I have discussed it, and we think it is the gentlest way to begin to bring you into society. Over time, there will be much curiosity, perhaps even a little gossip, so a little party like this will go some way to satisfying some of the curiosity. I won't lie to you, Jane, it's going to be a long road ahead. You have friends and family now, people who are on your side and always shall be. So, let's begin it all with a wonderful party."

As Jane got herself ready for the party, she could hardly take her eyes off her own appearance in the mirror. Fiona had helped her with her hair, not trusting one of the maids to do it lest a little jealousy crept in and they try to make a fool of Jane.

Having never had ringlets before, Jane just couldn't take her eyes off them. The very moment that Fiona had left her alone in the little bedroom that had been hers for the last few weeks, Jane had raced over to the long gilt framed oval mirror and looked at herself. She looked like a different girl altogether, a young woman. A young lady.

Already, Cora had had two dresses made for her, with two more underway with the seamstress. The dress she was wearing for the party was such a lovely shade of blue, the colour of cornflowers. It was nicely fitted with short sleeves and a modest neckline, and with the long white gloves covering the hands which still bore the roughness of a lifetime's work, Jane thought she looked quite the part. Even though she'd never been a vain girl, Jane decided to enjoy the moment as she turned this way and that, the fine fabric of her dress swirling about her ankles, revealing the satin slippers beneath. This was going to be a very fine party indeed.

Out of nowhere, Jane was suddenly transported in her mind back to Harry Newland's basement. She remembered the first moment she had seen the dirty, ragged little children, how they had wriggled with excitement when they had been given the smallest chunk of bread. She closed her eyes, feeling them stinging hot with tears; her vanity, however brief, had been crushed.

When Harry had been taken away by the peelers, Jane had been so worried about the children that she'd begged Cora and Fiona to do something. The authorities had searched for the children at the address Jane had given them in Southwark, but to no avail; all seven children had disappeared. Every time she wondered what had happened to them, it felt like a blow to the stomach. Perhaps, when she was finally settled with Cora and Edgar, she would set about searching for them. With that decision made, she might be better able to enjoy her party.

"I must say, you do look heavenly in that dress, Jane," Edgar said, never failing to surprise her with that boundless openness of his.

"Thank you," she said shyly, casting her eyes down for a moment. "You look very nice too," she went on, wondering if young ladies were supposed to complement young men in such a fashion.

He really did look nice, wearing his black trousers and smart black jacket and waistcoat with a white shirt and a lovely, pale green necktie holding his collars high and stiff about his neck. His dark hair looked thick and was smartly cut, his green eyes as beautiful as ever.

"Well, shall we dance?" Edgar asked brightly.

"Oh, no, I couldn't," Jane said, feeling a little panic-stricken.

"Why not? You don't have to worry about Mrs Prescott now, do you? What business is it of hers or anybody else if you and I choose to dance together?"

"It isn't that, Edgar," Jane said, feeling a little ashamed. "The thing is, I can't dance, I don't know how to. It's hardly the sort of thing they teach in the orphanage," she added and saw that Edgar instantly regretted his assumption.

"Oh, yes, of course, Jane, I really am so terribly sorry. I hope I didn't..."

"No, not at all," Jane said hurriedly, but she wanted to have a few minutes to herself. She knew she would have to get used to such embarrassments, as well as she knew that this was just the first in a long line. It made her feel a little tearful, and very much out of her depth. "Would you excuse me for just a minute, Edgar?" she said and smiled at him, seeing the sadness in his green eyes and knowing that he felt guilty.

"Yes, of course," he said and bowed like the gentleman he was before leaving her alone at the edge of the room.

Jane backed away further still, hiding away in the shadows and watching as everybody else enjoyed the party. There were people she didn't know, dancing, talking, eating. They were all enjoying her party, even though they didn't know her. But then they knew how to enjoy a party, didn't they? They knew what was expected of them, how to behave, how to dance, how to eat without making fools of themselves. Little Sally had once told her that she was neither fish nor fowl, and Jane realised that the same was still true today.

As if to make matters worse, her arm was suddenly gripped roughly, and she turned, with horror, to see that it was none other than Franklin Wakefield. The blue eyes which she had once thought full of mischief and merriment were cold and merciless as he glared down at her.

"They would have a party for *your sort* now, would they? I don't expect that any of the fine people here know that you were once flat on your back in the room above the Dog and Duck, do they?" He snarled at her.

"Let go of me, you're hurting my arm!" she said, wriggling to free herself, the memory of that awful day in Southwark coming back to her with full force.

"Perhaps I should tell them what you really are," he went on, and she realised from the dreadful stench of his breath, the awful fumes, that he was drunk. It gave her the greatest sense of danger that she had felt for weeks and weeks. Here was a man who was drunk and angry, a man who had received a letter from Cora Blythe demanding that he put an end to his nefarious activities immediately or she would go to the authorities. "You've all but ruined me! I needed that money, you jumped up little worm, I needed that money! Perhaps now I should make you pay. Perhaps I should tell a tale of my own; a tale I can add *anything* to and be believed. What do you say to that, Jane Ashford? How do you like my revenge?"

Fearing the inevitable humiliation, Jane used all her strength to free herself from the drunken man. She turned and ran from the room, hoping that nobody had seen her depart. Franklin Wakefield gave chase, catching her in the great hallway of the house, gripping her arm again and spinning her around to face him.

"Oh, no you don't, young *lady*," he said, adding mocking exaggeration to the word lady. "You are going to hear every bit of it. If I am going to suffer, so are you." He tried to drag her back in the direction of the party. However, Edgar Sinclair suddenly appeared, his green eyes flashing with anger.

"You get your hands off her this minute, Wakefield!" Edgar said and lunged for him, surprising him so that he immediately let go of his grip on Jane.

"What are you going to do about it? You're just a boy!" Wakefield said as Edgar landed a blow which sent him sprawling to the floor. Jane heard running footsteps and turned to see Mr Morton and two of the footmen racing along the corridor towards them.

It was all too much. As soon as the servants found out, everybody would find out. She couldn't bear it, not after everything she'd suffered so far. She had realised that it was going to be hard enough to be a part of their world, that privileged life of the upper classes. To have everything known now would be unbearable and she would much rather be away, go somewhere else, find work in service and stick to the only life she had ever known. As the struggle continued, Jane raced to the front door, opened it wide, and disappeared into the night.

Jane had only been running for five minutes when she realised that she had no idea where she was. With her tears blinding her, Jane had run through the alleyways into darker places; places that she had never even realised existed in her new and fine surroundings.

She heard footsteps running behind her, too exhausted to wonder if those footsteps had been following her all the way from the house.

With a sharp pain in her stomach from running, she began to slow down, she began to come to her senses.

Why had she run? Where was she really going to go in the middle of the night? The truth was, she was safe, wasn't she? Even if some gossip did make its way to the ears of others, she was safe. She hadn't killed a man; she wasn't on the run. With everything that she had put up with in her life, wasn't a little embarrassment the very least of it?

She stopped now, holding her side and breathing heavily. She was certain that it was Edgar who had followed her, and she turned, ready to face him: ready to apologise. However, the man who finally caught up with her was not Edgar Sinclair, but Harry Newland. Just as Jane opened her mouth to scream, he landed such a fierce blow on the side of her head that her world turned instantly black.

CHAPTER SEVENTEEN

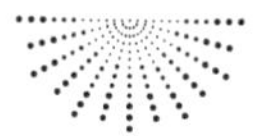

"So, how do you like my new place?" Harry Newland's face was just an inch from hers when she finally came to. She was underground, she could just sense it, in a cold, damp basement. With a gasp, she wondered if she was back in Southwark. "Gone upmarket now, haven't I? My new little lair right here in Covent Garden! Harry's gone up in the world. But then you'd have known that, wouldn't you, if I'd ever thought to give you such information. If I'd ever thought to trust you whilst you worked in that fancy house of yours, I'd have let you know that I'd moved my operation from the old place."

"Covent Garden? But aren't you supposed to be...?"

"He escaped from prison, didn't he, Jane!" came a little voice she recognised; it was Sally. "The peelers don't know where he is, and they're probably not really looking. Anyway, it doesn't take much to get out of prison if you give the jailers a few coins," she said, explaining in her own helpful little way.

Jane turned to look at her and could see that the child was pleased to see her. Despite the awful life she led, little Sally was still a child with all the innocence of a child. She didn't understand the world around her, and she didn't try. She just liked Jane and had clearly missed her.

"Sally," Jane said, feeling sick, her head throbbing where Harry had landed the vicious blow. She tried to move and realised then that she was tied rather tightly to an old wooden chair.

"You don't look half fancy in that dress, Jane. Where did you get it from?" Sally went on, and the rest of the children closed in around her, all keen to see just how fancy Jane looked.

"You're all right. You're all right, all of you" she said, so pleased to see the children again as tears ran down her face. "But you have to do something for me; you have to get me out of here," she said before Harry landed a fierce slap on her face. Sally gasped, and the rest of the children took a few steps backwards.

"You're going nowhere, girl. Harry Newland doesn't forget a betrayal like yours. As soon as I escaped from jail, I knew what I was going to do. I've been waiting and watching, Jane, just as I did for all those weeks whilst you were inside that house betraying me. I've been waiting for a moment like this. Imagine my surprise when I saw you running from that house in your posh frock like the devil was chasing you. What was it this time? Have you thrown another poor soul down the stairs then?"

"I have never killed anybody, Harry. But then you knew that all along, didn't you?" she said, staring at him with pure anger in her eyes.

"You can't blame a man for trying, can you? And anyway, didn't I once tell you that I'll do anything to survive? *Anything*, and I meant it. Now, what are you prepared to do to survive?"

"Nothing. I will do nothing more for you."

"Then it looks like you will stay strapped in a chair until you starve to death, girl," Harry said angrily.

Out of the corner of her eye, Jane could see Sally backing away, slowly inching her way across that evil basement to the door beyond.

"I don't care," Jane said, not really meaning it but doing anything she could to keep Harry's attention on her and off the slowly escaping Sally.

"Well, maybe you'll care about this," Harry said, his dark eyes glinting with spite in the gloom of the basement.

Jane watched as he crossed the room, her eyes adjusting to the gloom, focusing upon the wire crates. It was then that the oh so familiar sound of scratching and rummaging rats came back to her with full force. Harry reached up and took down one of the wire crates filled with his little devils. He walked across the room and stood in front of her, setting the crate down on the floor and opening it.

"Let's see how you feel about my little beauties crawling all over that fine dress of yours, that peachy skin. I'll stand here and watch whilst you scream yourself inside out, little miss hoity-toity. This is your end, and you're not going to like it. You'll wish you'd gone to the gallows rather than this, believe me," he said and reached in to take out the first rat.

Suddenly, the basement echoed with footsteps and Jane, her heart almost stopping with fear as she stared down at the rats, realised that Sally had run for help.

"You get off her, Harry Newland!" It was Sally's voice, Sally's screeching voice, and Sally's little foot which lashed out at the crouching man and knocked him clear off balance.

As Harry tried to get to his feet, he was knocked back down to the floor by none other than Edgar Sinclair. He was rescuing her for the second time that night.

The whole basement was suddenly full of peelers and Jane, still strapped to the chair, watched as Harry was taken away for the second time.

"Just make sure he doesn't escape from jail this time, would you?" Edgar called out irritably as they took him away.

Without another word, Edgar untied her from the chair, pulling her to her feet, and wrapping his arms around her.

"Why did you run, Jane? Why did you leave me?" he said, holding her so tightly that she felt protected from the world.

"I'm sorry, I'm so sorry. Mr Wakefield was going to tell everybody about me, he was going to say that I really had worked for him as he'd intended. I couldn't bear it. I knew I would never fit in if that happened."

"It's never going to happen, Jane. Wakefield let go of his senses for a moment in drink, but he's already coming to them now. Don't you worry, Aunt Cora has everything under control." He kissed the top of her head and Jane wrapped her own arms around his neck, finally clinging to him, finally discovering what it was like to fall in love.

CHAPTER EIGHTEEN

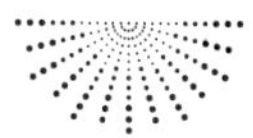

"Am I ever going to get that book back, Jane?" Edgar asked, dropping heavily into the armchair opposite the couch where she sat.

"No, never," Jane said, teasing him. "Never, never, never," she went on.

"How many times have you read it now?"

"Three."

"Then surely you must know the story inside out and back to front."

"Not really. You see, it's different every time. I mean it doesn't change, the story doesn't change, but my understanding of it does. Now that my reading and writing is improving, the world feels different."

"I do adore the way you say things, Jane."

"Oh, you mean my Cockney accent?"

"No, I wasn't talking about that, not that you have much of an accent to speak of anyway. No, I meant I like the way you put things. I like what you *say*, and I like how you *say it*. Really, I never met a girl who was so averse to simply accepting a compliment as you."

"You tease me so much I can hardly tell the compliments from the fooling," Jane said, and grinned at him.

In the six months that she had lived with Cora and Edgar, her whole world had changed. She felt comfortable now and safe, the two things which had eluded her for a lifetime.

Cora really did have everything under control, and not a squeak of gossip had got out at the party at Fiona Radcliffe's house. The guests had been told that Jane had become unwell and had retired to her room, and none of them ever discovered that she had run off into the night and had been discovered tied to a chair and about to be bitten to shreds by hungry rats.

As for Franklin Wakefield, Morton and the footman had, at Cora's insistence, locked the drunken man in the boot room below stairs. She had immediately dispatched Morton to collect Miss Emma Talbot's father, the Baron. It had been time to lay the cards on the table and have him do his part to help. He'd arrived at the party where he had been fully informed of all the circumstances by Cora, waiting until all the guests had finally gone home before Franklin Wakefield was released and suitably threatened by Lord Talbot himself. It was a threat of ruination so vehement that even in drink, Wakefield had believed it.

"I should think you've had enough adventure for one lifetime, Jane, without the need for Sir Walter Scott," Edgar went on, doing a very amusing display of mock exasperation. "But I can see I'm going to have to purchase myself another copy of *Ivanhoe*, aren't I?"

"No, we can share it, can't we?" Jane said and looked up at him for a moment from her book, grinning just as he did. "And I should think that you've had plenty of excitement now too, haven't you? I don't think there are many young men who have run into a rat catcher's lair and rescued a girl tied to a chair."

"No, I suppose not. Mind you, I could live another lifetime and never set eyes on another rat, thank you very much," he said and shuddered with some exaggeration.

"Then that makes two of us."

Of all her adventures, of all the ups and downs in her life in the last months, the thing which gave her the greatest sense of warmth and hope was the fact that the little children, Sally included, had been taken into proper care. Jane had been so insistent that they needed help that Cora had stepped in and, with Fiona's help, they had found the most suitable little orphanage, one that both ladies intended to become benefactors too. After all, they wanted to make sure that the brave little girl who had run for help without a thought to her own future was properly rewarded for her bravery. How better to have a say in how things were run than to denote a sizeable amount of money every year? The whole thing had given Cora and Fiona a new focus in life, and they had begun to devote more and more of their time to the good works of charity in all its forms.

Perhaps having such a close relative raised in poverty had opened even the kindly Cora Blythe's eyes a little wider to the suffering all around them.

"It really has been wonderful having you here, Jane. I think things must have been incredibly dull before you came into my life."

"Of course, they weren't dull, Edgar. You had your wonderful aunt, your friends."

"Yes, but I didn't have you, did I?" He was staring at her, his clear green eyes piercing the few yards between them.

Suddenly, he got to his feet and crossed the room, sitting down on the couch next to her. "I don't know if you've ever realised it, Jane Ashford, but I really am in love with you. I mean very much in love with you, the sort of *being in love* that has a chap wide awake half the night."

"I see," Jane said, and then began to laugh; what a silly thing to say! "I mean, I love you too, Edgar. I think I always have, but I was so afraid."

"But there's nothing to be afraid of anymore, is there?"

"No, I suppose not."

"May I kiss you?" he asked, with no hint of embarrassment, a broad smile on his face and his green eyes wide.

"Yes," she said and realised that she did feel a little afraid.

However, when he finally kissed her, every ounce of fear was dissolved. Every ounce of pain and suffering in her past evaporated into the ether, and she gave herself fully to that moment. It was brief, but there was some passion to it, a passion that she knew, deep in her heart, would grow as every day passed.

"As soon as you are sixteen, I intend to marry you," he said, that comical turn to his voice as evident as ever. "I do hope you don't mind very much."

"I don't mind at all, Edgar. I can't think of anything I'd like better." And with that, she closed her eyes and waited for him to kiss her again.

EPILOGUE

"I do look forward to Cora and Fiona coming to dinner, Edgar, don't you?" Jane said as she sat in front of her dressing table mirror and put the final touches to her hair.

"Yes, always. Even though we see them week in week out, I think I still miss them. I don't suppose that makes much sense, but you've been married to me long enough now to know that I don't often make sense," Edgar said and laughed. "I say, you look good enough to eat," he went on, sidling up to his wife, standing behind her and laying his hands on her shoulders.

"Behave yourself, Edgar, the children will be here in

a moment. You know how they like to hover about whilst we get ready."

"Yes, nosy little creatures!" he said and laughed, kissing the top of her head gently so as not to disarrange her hair. "You really are beautiful. You get more beautiful every day, my darling," his green eyes held hers, reflected in the mirror.

True to his word, Edgar had dropped down onto one knee on her sixteenth birthday and asked for her hand in marriage. Cora, who had seen the whole thing coming, obviously, had cried with joy, nonetheless. It would keep those she loved most close to her and, as far as she was concerned, it was just the right outcome.

Society had accepted Jane slowly, it was true, and there were many in it who would never accept her fully. The whole business of Franklin Wakefield was nothing but a distant memory and not a hint of it had ever escaped, thanks to Lord Talbot's intervention. Since it was his own daughter's careless choice of maid which had caused the whole catastrophe in the first place, he had felt rightfully a little responsible and had been keen to monitor the situation over the years. After all, if the gossip had ever escaped, his daughter would have also been tarnished.

It had taken a while for the cloud to disperse entirely. For the first couple of years of her new life, Jane had fully expected that somebody would hear something. But it had been almost ten years since that awful night at the party, the last time she had ever set eyes on Franklin Wakefield.

As for Maud Parsons, she had been turned out of Miss Talbot's service immediately. Despite her anger at Maud, Jane had been pleased to hear that Emma Talbot had written the girl a reference, likely as a means of buying her continued silence. Whilst Maud didn't truly deserve Jane's consideration, it was true that Jane was glad that she hadn't been forced to return to her old trade. Nobody deserved that, *nobody*.

Jane hadn't been at all surprised to hear that, during his first year of incarceration, Harry Newland had got into a fight with the wrong prisoner and had been killed. She hadn't been glad to hear of his passing, but she had to admit to a little relief. It wasn't for herself, but for all the vulnerable people who might have crossed his path in the years when he had become a free man again. Harry Newland was a predator, just like Franklin Wakefield in his own way. But unlike Wakefield, nobody would have been able to control Harry Newland.

"Here they come!" Edgar said and laughed as their son and daughter burst into the room, their nurse giving pointless chase.

"It's all right, Violet, they're just excited," Jane said and smiled.

"I do believe Mrs Blythe and Mrs Radcliffe have arrived, Ma'am," Violet said, smiling.

"Oh, good, then the children can have a few minutes with them before they go to bed." Jane smiled and ruffled Malcolm and Catherine's dark hair; Malcolm and Catherine, named for her mother and uncle, much to Cora's delight.

"Come on then, let's harass Aunt Cora and Aunt Fiona for a few minutes!" Edgar said. The children squealed with excitement as they followed their father out of the room.

"They have your hair, Edgar, but Jane's beauty. What a lovely combination!" Cora said as they all sat down to dinner. "I'm looking forward to a time when they're old enough to sit down to dinner with us, they're so lovely and bright."

"Oh, yes, they are," Fiona added.

"Well, it will be a while yet. Malcolm is only six and Catherine five. Their table manners are worse than mine were at that age," Jane said, and they all laughed.

"Oh, now I have some wonderful news for you!" Fiona said, smiling brightly at Jane.

"Oh, yes, do tell her!" Cora was equally excited.

"Guess who has come to my home as our newest maid?"

"Who, Fiona?" Jane asked, feeling a little flutter of excitement; she had a feeling she knew what was coming.

"Little Sally! She is seventeen years old; can you believe it?" Fiona went on.

"And the last to leave the orphanage, isn't she?" Edgar said, as interested in Cora and Fiona's charitable works as Jane was.

"That is a condition of our substantial patronage, Edgar. No child turned out whilst still a child." Cora looked at Jane, and Jane knew she was thinking of her own hard start, of being sent into service at just twelve.

"Things are changing, bit by bit. I say it's all down to fine ladies like the two of you," Edgar said and reached for his glass. "Men bark and bluster, but it is the ladies who change things. Let's have a toast!" he went on, his wonderful brightness making Jane love him more and more.

"Yes, let's," Jane said and reached for her glass, raising it and looking to her handsome husband to make the toast.

"To the ladies! To the wonderful ladies who improve the world!"

"To the ladies," the three women chorused.

"And to my darling wife," Edgar went on, surprising

Jane. "Whom I shall love for all eternity," he lowered his voice and stared at her.

"To Jane!" Cora and Fiona gladly toasted her.

With her world complete, Jane Sinclair knew that she had so much to be thankful for. Her old life had shaped her new life in a way that she would always be grateful for. Without the past, there was no present.

"Thank you, Edgar. Thank you all," Jane said and dashed a tear of happiness from the corner of her eye. Love, family, laughter, it was all anyone could ask for.

Thanks for Reading

I love sharing my Victorian Romances with you and have several more waiting for my editor to approve.

I would love to invite you to join my exclusive Newsletter, you will be the first to find out when my books are available. It is FREE to join, and I will send you The Foundling's Despair FREE as a thank you.

Read on for a preview of The Lost Nightingale

I want to thank you so much for reading this book. Read on for a sneak preview of The Lost Nightingale

You can find all my books on Amazon, click the yellow follow button and Amazon will let you know when I have new releases and special offers.

THE LOST NIGHTINGALE PREVIEW

Anna Bailey crept through the hushed crowd. She was small enough to ease her way, weaving back and forth, without causing a fuss. It was easy when Lucy Lawrence was flying through the air; the crowd were too mesmerised to pay much heed to the scruffy girl sneaking her way to the front.

The big top of *Gerrity's Unbelievable Show* was average for a travelling circus of their standard. It was large enough to accommodate seating for those who could afford a few extra coins to sit in comfort, with a pit area for the masses who couldn't. Anna always crept through the pit area. If she tried to wander through the seating, Mr Gerrity might have seen her and lost his famous temper; famous among the performers, at any rate. For anyone paying to see the show, Mr Gerrity was a fine-looking man with a big sense of humour and an even bigger laugh. It seemed that everything, absolutely everything, was a part of the show, even Mr Gerrity's character.

Finally, Anna could see what she had come to see. Lucy, her knees hooking her to the bar of the trapeze, her arms spread wide, flew through the air. The crowd all looked up as one, reminding Anna of the countless times she'd watched migrating birds turning together. She'd always wondered what force drew them to act in unison. Of course, looking at the tipped heads of all around her, Anna needn't wonder why. Lucy was a true wonder, and as far as Anna was concerned, the star of the show.

"With no safety net, she flies high above the treacherous ground, that earth ready and waiting to swallow her up!" Mr Gerrity roared, whipping the crowd up into a frenzy.

Anna despised his additions to what should have simply been a thing of beauty. She despised the way he dangled death as a possibility; a possibility the audience lapped up like thirsty dogs.

There was so much to be admired in the performers. Their skill was second to none, defying gravity and even their own bodies to provide a thing of wonder for others to admire. But Anna knew that this wasn't why they were here. Not even the seated ones who had a few extra coins and thought themselves so much better. No, the truth was, they'd all come hoping to see something awful. They were the same sort of people who would have been entertained by public executions.

"One false move and the Flying Fairy will plummet to the earth, smashed to smithereens!" Gerrity bellowed, and the crowd drew in their breath as Lucy, her white-blonde ponytail streaming beneath her like a canary's wing swung higher and higher. All the time, building speed and momentum.

It was an apt description; at just seventeen, Lucy resembled a sweet fairy when her feet were on the ground. In the air, even more so, for her skill in the twists and turns was something of a miracle as she seemed to hover or fly at will.

Holding on with slim, fragile-looking arms, she rolled her body and let go to a gasp of the crowd. Tucking, she twisted in the air as strong and graceful as an eagle on the wing. There was not a sound as she turned and flew an impossible distance to the waiting trapeze that had been swung at just the right moment for her to catch. None of the crowd had noticed it before she grabbed hold and they let out a great sigh of awe.

Lucy's nimble fingers hooked on to the bar, and she unfurled into a beautifully neat, taut straight line as the complicated manoeuvre was complete.

The crowd breathed again, perhaps with a hint of disappointment.

Anna wondered if she were just a little jaded. Could you be jaded at thirteen? She'd been raised in the circus and knew nothing else, and she'd watched crowd after crowd silently willing catastrophe to do its worst. It had, of course, from time to time, and Anna had seen eyes wildly alight with mawkish glee even as the lips proclaimed the awfulness of the whole thing; the tragedy of it. But people loved tragedy. Tragedy was what they were paying to see whether they admitted it to themselves or not.

Of course, there was always tragedy, even if there was not an accident. For the most part, the tragedy displayed daily was the tragedy of birth. The deformed children who had grown up to discover that the only work on offer was to make a mockery of themselves and their lives as circus sideshows. For instance, the pinheaded man, his head so small that his body looked horribly wide. Anna felt her heart break every time she looked at him, yet all he ever did was smile. With his brain unable to develop within the constricted walls of so small a skull, he didn't have enough wits to know he was being stared at, mocked, and humiliated. Perhaps that was the only mercy in all of it.

Then there were the women with extraordinary facial and body hair. They seemed to be in constant supply, and she often wondered how it was Mr Gerrity found them. For the most part, the ladies didn't speak a word of English, and she'd never dared to ask where they came from. Circus men always seemed to be able to find the vulnerable; they had a sense for them, a natural talent for drawing them in.

"Our beautiful Flying Fairy lives to fly another day!" Mr Gerrity called out loudly. "But don't forget, we're here all week, ladies and gentlemen. Every day at the circus is different from the day before!" He always grew louder when he tried to tempt them back to spend their coins again.

Anna groaned inwardly. It would have been more honest of him to shout, *"Come back tomorrow, and maybe she really will fall next time!"*

Lucy had flown to the platform high above the crowd, stepping onto it as if it were on the ground. No nerves showed, there was no hint of anything other than the easiest balance. She let go of the trapeze and stood on the tiny platform. She looked beautiful in her skin-tight bodysuit. It was lilac and shone like silk, fine net wings attached to the sleeves, wings which flew when Lucy did. It was an outfit that would only ever be acceptable in the circus, not in the normal 1883; not in the England outside of the big top where hems were low and necklines impossibly high.

Lucy waved to the crowd; even that simple gesture was filled with balance and grace.

Anna waved back, knowing that Lucy probably couldn't even see her there. She waved because she was grateful; grateful for a few minutes of escape into a world where it was possible to fly.

"And now, the most amazing trick rider in England, the one and only Bernard Bailey!" Mr Gerrity roared, and the crowd let their attention wander away from the Flying Fairy as she climbed down the rope ladder to safety and prepared themselves for the appearance of Anna's father.

Even as Bernard Bailey flew out into the ring, the clattering of his horse's hooves loud enough to be heard over the musicians' sudden and wild playing, Anna turned away and eased back through the crowd and out of the big top.

Anna had prepared everything for the evening meal early that day and had only to warm it all through. She had a fire alight outside the high sided carriage that she and her father both lived and travelled in. Setting up a metal tripod, she hung the pan containing the rich stew above the flames.

Anna had already eaten her meal earlier, knowing that her father wouldn't care if she sat down to eat with him or not. The truth was, on the first night in a new town, Lucy was always too nervous to eat much as the night went on. Her sense of anxiety simply increased as she cooked and listened to the roar of the crowd inside the big top as they watched the amazing Bernard Bailey charging around the edge of the ring standing on his horse's back. She wondered if they would be so amazed by him if they'd seen how cruelly he treated his horses? If they knew what it took to make performers out of the poor creatures. She shook her head, she knew them, all of them, even though they'd never been introduced. She knew them well enough to know that they wouldn't care one way or the other. People who drew such pleasure from the very sight of the unfortunately born, the prospect of a woman falling to her death, or a beautiful wild animal forced to act against its every instinct, wouldn't care at all about beaten and broken horses.

"I saw you in the crowd today," Lucy said, walking towards her with a bright smile.

"Did you really?" Anna was amazed that a woman who needed every shred of concentration to work the trapeze could spare an ounce of it to look for the starstruck little girl who admired her so.

"At the end, when I was standing on the platform. I could see you waving at me." Lucy grinned and sat down on the grass beside Anna as she continued to keep an eye on the stew. "Making his dinner then?" she went on.

"Yes, I managed to get a little meat, so he should be happy for that much," Anna said and shrugged. She knew it was unlikely that her father would give her a word of praise about the meal she'd made for him. After all, she didn't get a word of praise for keeping the wooden carriage they lived in clean and orderly, his clothes laundered, his hair cut just the way he liked it, his chin freshly shaved. Surely, it would be easier to look after a baby.

"Are any of them ever happy about anything? I mean..." Lucy had begun conversationally, but her voice trailed away to nothing and Anna followed her gaze. She shouldn't have been surprised to see her father leaning one arm against one of the circus wagons, a young and adoring woman with her back against it looking up at him.

"It's always the same, Lucy. The first night in any town, he always picks up with somebody. I don't know how he does it; look, he's so much older than she is." Anna tried to bite back her disgust.

"Some women like it." Lucy shrugged. "It doesn't matter what he looks like or how old he is, for ten minutes he was the star of the show. I don't understand it myself, but women will throw themselves at any man at all if he was the centre of attention for a while, if all eyes were on him."

"I just wish he'd go somewhere else to... well..." Anna was too embarrassed to finish the sentence. Even though Lucy must surely have realised that Bernard Bailey's conquests were always made in the same little carriage where his daughter was trying to sleep, still, Anna couldn't admit it out loud.

"Why don't you come to me? Look, hand me out your blankets now before he gets here and come over to me as soon as you've finished feeding him. He looks engrossed enough, I'm sure he won't miss you if you sleep in my carriage."

"I'm sure he won't miss me either," Anna said sadly.

"I wish I hadn't said it quite like that, my sweet," Lucy said and put a long, slender arm around Anna's shoulders. "I suppose it's just the life we lead here, isn't it? Never settled anywhere, travelling all the way up the country only to turn around and travel all the way back down again. I suppose, in his own way, your father is lonely."

"I just wish he would go and be lonely in somebody else's carriage," Anna said and shuddered. "It's impossible to sleep when..." Again, she couldn't finish her sentence.

"This is a hard life, no doubt about it. I was born in a circus, Anna, just like you. Only, my father made me train as an acrobat and then a trapeze artist. There was never any choice in it, and he used to pick up women along the way. I understand how you feel," she went on in a soothing voice.

"You're so good at it, Lucy. Don't you like it?"

Lucy's eyes dropped to stare at the ground. There was a desolation about her that Anna had never seen before.

"I hate being here. I hate that I never learned anything else in my life but this." Lucy spread her bird-like arms, and for a moment, Anna thought she would fly away and hover before her like a fairy tale fairy. Of course, she didn't.

"You always look so content on the trapeze."

"It is the only time I *am* content. Being in the middle of the show, Mr Gerrity is not able to bawl and shout and throw things if he doesn't like what he sees. I forget they're all there; Gerrity and his wife, the crowd, everybody. It's the only time I feel free... when I'm flying. But then, like any captive bird, my wings are pushed back down against my body and I'm stuffed back inside the cage." Lucy's beautiful face looked so sad that Anna could have cried; her bright blue eyes, her impossibly pale blonde hair, everything about her so beautiful and for what? So that she could live a life without any choice at all.

"Come on then, hand down those blankets, and I'll go and hide them in my carriage. And come to me when you're ready, Anna, don't wait around," Lucy said, forcing herself to speak more brightly and kissing the top of Anna's head.

ALSO BY JESSICA WEIR

I would love to invite you to join my exclusive Newsletter, you will be the first to find out when my books are available. It is FREE to join, and I will send you The Foundling's Despair FREE as a thank you.

Also available on Amazon:

The Lost Nightingale

The Mill Daughter's Courage

You can find all my books on Amazon, click the yellow follow button and Amazon will let you know when I have new releases and special offers.

This story is a work of fiction any resemblance to people, living or dead, is purely coincidence. All places, names, events, businesses, etc. are used in a fictional manner. All characters are from the imagination of the author.

Printed in Great Britain
by Amazon

55209723R00156